Ten Kings

Ashok K. Banker's internationally acclaimed and bestselling Ramayana Series is credited with having launched the new wave of Indian mythological epics in English, currently the country's most popular genre. His Epic India Library is a Lifetime Writing Plan to retell all the major myths, legends and itihasa of the Indian subcontinent in one massive interlinked story-cycle. His 42 books have sold over 2 million copies in 16 languages and 57 countries worldwide. *Ten Kings* marks the beginning of his Itihasa Series, retelling key events from Indian recorded history. It will be followed shortly by the sequels *Harappa* and *Mohenjo-Daro*. His two-film adaptation of the *Mahabharata* is being produced by Disney.

TEN KINGS

*Based on the historical battle of Dasarajna
in the Rig Veda*

ASHOK K. BANKER

AMARYLLIS

AMARYLLIS

Copyright © Ashok K. Banker 2014

This edition first published in 2014
Second impression 2014

AMARYLLIS

An imprint of **Manjul Publishing House Pvt. Ltd.**
7/32 Ground Floor, Ansari Road, Daryaganj,
New Delhi 110 002
Email: amaryllis@amaryllis.co.in
Website: www.amaryllis.co.in

Registered Office:
10, Nishat Colony, Bhopal 462 003 - India

Distribution Centres:
Ahmedabad, Bengaluru, Bhopal, Kolkata, Chennai,
Hyderabad, Mumbai, New Delhi, Pune

ISBN: 978-93-81506-54-7

Cover Art: Kunal Kundu

Printed and Bound in India by
Thomson Press (India) Ltd.

The song belongs to they who listen.

वि स्द्यो विश्वा दृंहितान्य् एषाम् इन्द्रः पुरः सहसा सप्त दर्दः ।
व्य् आनर्वस्य तृत्सवे गयम् भाग् जेष्म पुरं विदथे मृध्रवाचम् ॥ ७ ०१८ १३
नि गव्यवो अनवो द्रुह्यवश् च षष्टिः शता सुषुपुः षट् सहस्रा ।
षष्टिर् वीरासो अधि षड् दुवोयु विश्वेद् इन्द्रस्य वीर्या कृतानि ॥ ७ ०१८ १४

~Mandala 7, Rig Veda~

	raja vai rajasuyenestva bhavati	
	samrat vajapeyena avaram	
	hi rajyam param samrajyam	

The Rajaka who offers the Rajasuya becomes Rajan,
The Rajan who offers the Vajapeya becomes Samrat,
Samrat is always higher than the Rajan.

~Satapatha Brahmana (V.1.1.12-13)~

Author's Note

The 7th Mandala of the Rig Veda tells us of a battle called Dasarajna, which literally translates as Ten Kings.

In reverential terms, the Sanskrit verses describe a conflict in which ten major tribal chiefs or kings sought to displace and destroy Raja Sudas of the Trtsu Bharatas tribe.

The ten kings were organised and led by Anu, rajan of the tribe of the same name, and Anu in turn was guided by his preceptor Vishwamitra. As with many Vedic names, it's impossible to tell whether this Vishwamitra and his counterpart Vashishta, Sudas's guru, were the same brahmarishis whose legendary feud appears in other puranic works. Since collective names were common in those times, it's possible that their names represent their tribe or varna, rather than specific individuals.

The ten kings themselves are listed in the Rig Veda and described as being allies of the Trtsu Bharatas who were instigated by Anu into turning against Sudas and invading his territory with the sole intention of destroying him and his tribe and claiming their land.

The land in question was the rich alluvial plain we now know as the Punjab.

Specifically, the land bordered by the Ravi and Beas rivers, or Parusni as it was then called.

As a fertile and rich land, it was a great prize, particularly in that era when the nomadic tribes of Western Asia and the sub-continent were moving from a hunter-gatherer economy to an agricultural one.

The site also had a strategic significance: It was the threshold of the sub-continent itself and whichever power controlled that region, could control access to the treasures and wonders of the world's most fabled land, desired and sought by conquerors and cultures across the western world.

The reasons leading up to the Dasarajna battle are not detailed in the Rig Veda but are easy to deduce. As with most armed conflicts, it's likely there were multiple reasons, some economic, or political, or even personal ones for the assault.

In any case, on a stormy day during the height of the rainy season, the ten kings chose to launch an all-out assault against Sudas and his small but strong tribe of Trtsu Bharatas, surrounding them with forces so superior that the only possible outcome would be decimation.

The sheer size and nature of the invading army suggests that their intention was not merely to possess the land but to destroy Sudas and the Trtsu Bharatas, which means that personal animosity must have played a major part in their assault.

The Rig Veda tells us that the army of the ten kings consisting of over sixty thousand men arrayed in four-fold akshohini formation – infantry, cavalry, chariot, and elephant – assembled on the banks of the Parusni river and were met with a force of Trtsu Bharatas on foot and horseback numbering less than a tenth of that figure.

Sixty thousand heavily armed men, accompanied by armoured war elephants, chariots, horse and foot soldiers versus a force of less than six thousand on horse and foot.

The result was a foregone conclusion.

Vastly outnumbered and outmatched, Sudas should

logically have surrendered or fled.

By doing so, he could have saved himself and his people, either fleeing to other safer regions or choosing life as dasyas (slaves).

He did neither.

What manner of king stands and fights such impossible odds?

What manner of man takes on impossible odds and stands his ground?

Clearly, Sudas was no ordinary kshatriya.

The fact that he chose not to flee suggests two things: One, he was proud and strong and believed it was his dharma to fight, even if it meant certain death. Two, he had an ace up his sleeve.

My expansion and retelling of that section of Rig Veda chooses to believe both points.

The Rig Veda spends several shlokas extolling Sudas's virtues and his achievement in that historic battle. Even in an age given to epic hyperbole, the 7th Canto of Rig Veda stands out for its eulogies to Sudas, his people, the legendary nature of the conflict and the extraordinary victory.

What happened on that rainy day on the banks of the Parusni?

How did Raja Sudas defeat the ten kings and their far superior army?

Why did he even try?

What was Thundergod Indra's role in the battle, and was it a literal or metaphorical one?

What actually happened and how did it play out on that rain-swept field?

These are some of the questions I seek to answer in *Ten Kings*.

Not through an essay or through conjecture, because I'm not a historian. But through a recreation of the events leading up to, during and immediately after the Battle of Ten Kings.

As with any historical novel, I've invented dialogue, detail and narrative connections that help bring to life the period, the people, the conflict, the culture.

But most of all, I've tried to bring alive the events of that day. To set the characters and events in motion and let them unfold before you as if they were happening right now, before your senses.

So we can go back in time and relive the battle in all its vivid and intense detail.

And attempt to bring one of the most dramatic and seminal moments in India's life story out of the dusty corners of the history books into living, fighting, full-blown sentience.

Turn the page. Watch the past come alive.

And make a stand with Sudas and his Trtsu Bharatas on that rainy day by the Parusni.

I did and it was quite an experience. Now it's your turn.

Happy Reading!

Ashok K. Banker
Andheri, Mumbai
4 March 2014

KAAND 1

1

THE LAST watch of the night, just before dawn. Awake without remembering when he had woken or why.

The sky above, a tent of black silk stained red in the far corner, as if from a bloodstain that had failed to wash clean. The stain seeped farther as he watched. What name might a painter put to that particular shade of red? Vermillion, crimson, scarlet, ochre…? To his un-artistic kshatriya eyes, it was blood red.

His father had called a sky that colour a Warrior's Sky.

When he had asked why, his father had cuffed him with rough affection and said that some day his insolent son would go to war for himself, see the light of burning villages turn the horizon crimson and know what a Warrior's Sky meant. Until then, his father had added with a guffaw, he would have to settle for staring at a horse's rump. The other warriors had snorted into their cups of soma and continued the days' long revelry that followed a battle. Sudas would grow up to recall many such revelries; they were among the only times his father permitted him to be with the warriors, and to stay close to him.

He lay on his pallet, hands behind his neck, gazing up at the night sky. Stars still gleamed like dirty diamonds embedded in coal. Finally, knowing he could sleep no more, he rose and stretched in preparation for the yogic exercise routine he executed each day on waking, since he was a boy. It was based on his guru Brahmarishi Vashishta's philosophical and religious outlook and Sudas often thought of it as the Yoga Vashishta technique. The exercise helped clear his mind of the detritus of half-remembered dreams and palliate any residues of nightmares. There were more of the latter than the former these days.

As a boy, he had often wondered at the need to perform these difficult asanas. Now, as he aged and matured, it worked as a release from the burdens and responsibilities of being a husband, father and chief.

He was sweating as he drew to a close. The black silk tent of night had caught fire in the east and golden flames licked their way upwards over the ranges. Far to the west, the silvery strand of the Parusni began to twinkle as it caught the first light and he felt a sudden surge of pride – all the lands he could see from here to that river's banks were Bharata lands.

And I am king of this domain I survey.

It was a sobering thought and as he moved to a cross-legged asana and becalmed himself, he wondered if being king, or *rajan* as the Trtsus called it in Sanskrit, was the same for all men. Had it been the same for his father? The hoary guffawing face with its shiny battle scars and cracked teeth loomed large in the lightening sky, and Sudas knew that his father may have accepted the title of Rajan for political reasons, but in private he spat on such pomposity.

'Better to be a man and respected like a king, than to be a king respected by no man,' Pijavana had often said. He had been contemptuous of politicking and the endless debates in sabhas and samitis. He was a man most at home with a sword in his hand and a horse between his legs, riding out to war.

In fact, his father's one-path life ambition had been simply to live and die a warrior. Anything else was politics or matronising, he would have added, smashing his empty cup to underline his point. Chief Pijavana had loved smashing his cups, though only after he was done drinking from them.

2

IT WAS still dark outside. The palace complex was quiet as Sudas walked across the muddy central courtyard, churned up by a thousand pairs of hooves and uks cart wheels.

The wedding the night before had kept everyone up late. Even the sentries had been permitted to relax their vigil and sleep off their indulgences. There were almost a score of visiting kings and their entourages ensconced in the palace complex right now. The complex itself was a gated enclave situated on a strategic part of the grama and occupying an entire quarter of it. It comprised one score and five great halls, each with the capacity to accommodate two score persons comfortably. As he walked from his own residence all the way across the long rectangular courtyard, he glanced up. Even in the darkness, the krtadhvaj – embroidered gaily coloured cloth banners proclaiming the tribe of its owner – hung limply outside each great hall he passed, indicating the kinship of its present occupants. All but two of the halls had a banner outside, and he had spent the night in one of the unclaimed halls to gain a few hours of privacy. Each visiting king's retinue included a company of his own personal guard, numbering close to a thousand armed men in the royal enclave alone. These were not merely the kings' guards but yoddhas – the most distinguished champions in the tribe. Only a suicidal fool would dream of attacking the Trtsu capital right now.

In any case, he mused with the trace of a smile on his face, there was nobody left to attack! The most powerful kings in the known world were right here, under his roof. Or roofs, to be precise.

He passed the last of the great halls and turned right, towards the northern corrals. As he turned the corner, the scent of horse, elephant and uksan invaded his nostrils. The yogic exercises always primed his senses to preternatural alertness and he had found that scent could be trusted to reveal potential danger far more effectively than sight or sound. The animal part of the mortal mind knows the scent of fear; creatures about to attack, inflict violence or harm always experience great fear, caused by the most basic instinct of self-preservation – rage and anger are merely perversions of that fear. He had found that by trusting the instinctive reactions of the primitive part of his brain, he could utilise the sense of smell to know when danger lurked. An ambush party could render itself invisible, assassins could lie in wait without making a single sound, but the scent of fear could never be concealed. It was a trick he had learned from his dogs.

Speaking of which, he missed his faithful hounds. They would all be sleeping in the main hall, with his children and wife and her personal retinue of women bodyguards and serving maids. He had left the hounds there to serve as an additional level of protection. The visiting kings were all friends and allies, but anything was possible when a thousand warriors got drunk together, especially given the long, complex, often bloody history of internecine conflicts, tribal disputes and clan wars. He had not wanted to take any chances, the hounds were a precaution. The matrix of the pack, a great mastiff-hound hybrid named Sarama, had sat facing the door as he shut it, her eyes gleaming in the flickering torchlight. He had no doubt that he would find her lying in the same position when he opened that door again, ready to leap up and tear out the throat of any intruder. Already she would know from his scent that he was awake and abroad and would be awaiting him eagerly, even as her inbred discipline kept her at her post. He smiled, looking forward to seeing her happy snout when he pushed open the great wooden doors.

But first he wanted to wash and slake his thirst. And his goal was to do that without waking his family or guests or even his serving boys and girls, who deserved their rest like everyone else. That was why he was headed for the northern corral.

He passed around the corner of the northernmost great hall without pausing. There was no danger here. Just the normal bracing odours of assorted animal offal. Ah, he loved the smell of horseshit in the morning; it reminded him that he was alive.

There were half a thousand head in the northern corral alone and they whinnied and whickered sleepily as his scent reached them, not alarmed, merely passing on the word that mortals were around.

His own private steeds, three score head or so, fenced in a separate smaller corral just off the large one, bobbed their heads in greeting. He hesitated, weighing his need to slake his thirst with his love for his steeds, and decided to look in on them first. He leaned over the wooden fence as they crowded around him, nuzzling, pushing, nosing, snuffling, and expressing their affection in the unselfconscious way that only animals can. Saryu, the large white mare he favoured, grew impatient and began pushing the others away when she sensed them growing too familiar. She was always a matron to them, not just figuratively but literally too, having served as dam to at least five of them and as mate to another three.

He pushed them away at last, patting Saryu firmly, then turned towards the large trough that the sarathis would have freshly filled the night before, regardless of how drunk or sober they were. There was never a reason not to keep fresh feed and water for the animals, not in Trtsu lands. The trough lay in pitch darkness in the lee of the northernmost great hall and he found it by foreknowledge alone, feeling his way along the fence.

He dipped his hands into the cool wetness of the trough, raised them to his face in the darkness and sniffed at the water. His horses had been drinking from it but it was still fresh enough for his purposes:

He had washed in far murkier waters and suffered no harm. Horse, dog, uksan, mortals, all who lived and worked together were entitled to eat and drink together as well. It was the Trtsu way. Nay, it was the natural way.

He stripped naked, using water liberally, washing off the sweat and cooling his heated muscles. The water was greatly refreshing – he barely hesitated a moment before drinking freely from it. Over in his private corral, his horses whinnied encouragingly, as if saying, *Go on, go on, then, and drink up to your stomach's content. What's ours is yours as well, Chief!*

'Thank ye, thank ye, kindly,' he chuckled as he finished. The thought of thanking his horses for having drunk their water was an amusing one and he suddenly found himself suppressing a surge of laughter. It made him choke on a mouthful of water and he coughed, hawked, spat and then thumped the side of the trough. The timber rang dully.

'Fascinating,' said a voice behind his left shoulder. 'A king laughing at nothing as he bathes in a horse trough.'

In a flash, Sudas found his sword, turned and with a single motion pointed the blade at the invisible speaker.

3

THE DARKNESS beneath the overhang was absolute. Even Sudas's keen sight could not penetrate the veil of shadows that masked the speaker. He kept his sword hand outstretched, ready to make a move at the first sign of threat.

'Who lurks like a craven in the darkness?' he asked, his voice level. There was no need to rouse the whole palace complex. Most of the wedding party would have fallen asleep only an hour or so earlier. He himself had gone to bed barely three hours before he woke up again. 'Come out, show yourself.'

A soft chuckle issued from a spot where the shadows were deepest, gathered together like a cloak folded upon itself. It was a moonless night, and the starlight, diamond-bright until a little while ago, was dimmed by the spreading glow in the east. All Sudas could see were the outline and structure of the northern great hall and aspects of its timber beams and pillars, and the ground beneath his feet, with its red clay mud, the rich alluvial soil of the Five Rivers plain.

Slowly, like a form coalescing from a swirling mist, a man emerged into the open, from the deep shadows of the overhang. He was tall and powerfully built; from the depth his heels sank to in the yielding mud, Sudas could make out that he was heavier than most men. His head was large in proportion to his body. Deep-pitted shadows masked his features, although his eyes glinted within their sockets, under heavy brows.

Even before the man raised his bearded face to let the last vestiges of starlight catch his features, Sudas was quite certain he knew who it was.

Anu, the eponymous chieftain and king of the Anu, perhaps the most powerful tribe sharing space with the Trtsu Bharatas upon the Parusni plain.

'You are wrong to assume that the one who lurks in darkness is a craven, Sudas,' said the king of the Anu. 'Indeed, it is the hunter who moves by darkness, depriving both himself and his prey the benefit of vision, and reducing the hunt to a game of instinct, wit and skill.'

Sudas lowered the sword the instant he recognised Anu's face. To have let it stay up even an instant longer would have suggested he feared Anu. Among yoddhas, even a sign of weakness that miniscule was dishonourable. A true yoddha turned his back even when the enemy had a strung arrow pointed at him. That was the kshatriya way – to trust completely in the code of dharma, and never fear death or pain. *Dharma before dishonour*, as Chief Pijavana used to say. He did exactly that, setting down the sword and continuing his ablutions even as he continued speaking over his shoulder.

'And what is it you hunt here at this hour? Does the king of the Anu lack suitable prey in his own lands that he needs come to my palace complex, in the heart of my grama, in order to find good game?'

The barb struck home. He sensed Anu fall still for a fraction longer than was needed, then sensed that the man forced himself to chuckle softly and disregard the comment. The Anu were known for their sense of pride and intolerance for criticism.

'Hunting takes many forms, King Sudas,' he said. 'And if it is good game you desire, the Anu possess enough to keep you in sporting health for the rest of your life. Although it would be best if you refrained from dipping your snout into their drinking pools!'

This time the chuckling seemed more genuine as he laughed at Sudas's expense. Sudas did not mind it. He had learned a long time ago from a very wise man that insults, sneers and curses only distorted the faces of those who hurled them, while they did nothing to hurt those they were aimed at – unless you allowed them to hurt you. If you were not offended, even the grossest insult was ineffectual.

'I cannot promise that,' he said now in response. 'For the truth is, I love all living beings of all species and to me, dipping my snout in a lion's pool, a horse's trough, or a dog's bowl, is no different from drinking soma with kings such as Anu!'

Sudas straightened up and turned around, his washing done.

The sky had lightened only marginally but he found himself able to make out the other man's face a little more clearly. The expression of pure unmasked rage was a revelation. It was the face of a man who would kill him on the spot, without a second's hesitation. As it was, Anu had his fist upon the pommel of the sword tied at his waist and that fist was tight, judging from the tension in the shoulder above it.

Come now, Sudas, you just compared him to an animal! What did you expect? He is an Anu after all.

Sudas waited for the fist to draw the sword and for the man to make his move. But it never happened.

With a final searing glare, Anu turned on his heel and strode away with large angry strides. He turned the corner of the northern great hall and was gone from sight.

Sudas hefted his own sword, which he had discretely taken hold of as he turned around, just in case Anu's comments about hunting had been something more than mere wordplay. One could never be absolutely certain with the Anu. After all, there had been that ugly dispute over river rights to the Parusni just the previous autumn. And what had the man been doing, lurking in the darkness at this ungodly hour, staring out at the northern corral?

Hunting, he had said.

So what had he been hunting? Who was his intended prey?

Sudas shook his head, thinking that it was unlikely he would ever find out. If there was one thing the Anu were famous for – or notorious, if you preferred – it was their legendary discretion. Silent, deadly gossip, like the barely audible hiss of a serpent about to strike. It was not even a criticism; the Anu themselves hailed the serpent's sibilant reticence as a virtue to be emulated. Even if Anu had been willing to tell him what purpose had brought him here at such an hour after the head-splitting revelries and excesses of the night before, Sudas thought that his neighbour and fellow king would hardly reveal that purpose now, after their little clash of wits.

4

SARAMA LEAPED up with a woeful bark. Her glossy brindly coat rippled over powerful muscles as she surged forward, leaping at him with unchecked delight. The other dogs took to their feet as well, barking in consternation. Sudas laughed as his favourite companion stood up to place her forepaws possessively upon his chest and proceeded to give him a good thrashing with her tongue. She punctuated the rough licking with little yelps of complaint, protesting at his leaving her the night before.

'Yes, yes, I know,' he said, ruffling her fur vigorously to reciprocate her intensity, 'you always go where I go. But last night I needed you to be here, to keep my family safe. It's because I trust you over all others, even more than I would trust my own kind. Do you ken?'

She woofed deeply once to show that she

understood and had done as he had commanded. Dropping back on all fours, she turned to trot away, looking back over her shoulder to make sure he followed. When she saw him wasting time fussing over the other dogs – who were noisily complaining that he always gave too much attention to their matrix and not enough to them – she barked once, admonishing him to get a move on.

'Yes, Maatr, I'm coming,' he said, laughing as he pushed his way through the pack and followed her. 'By Indra, you're a bossy one!'

Each of the great halls was built precisely the same way with the finest timber logs from the high mountains. These were rolled downriver, then carted to the grama by elephants and uks working together. The basic structure was a simple rectangle with a flat timber terrace topped by a sloping thatched roof to deflect the monsoon rains and occasional hail or sleet. The great doors opened inwards in keeping with the Arya belief that, were the gods to visit, they must never need to pause or step back before entering a domicile.

Immediately within the doors was a vestibule for stowing weapons, discarding dirty boots, saddles, armour and sundry accoutrements that one did not wish to bring into the house. Beyond the vestibule lay the main hall itself, long and wide, with vaulting ceilings five times a man's height. In the centre of the hall was the yagna square, a sacred space reserved for Agni, Lord of Fire, with a flue chute going up through a hole in the roof. Around this were arranged an assortment of seats in varying sizes and shapes, made from pieces of timber left over from the construction of the main structure. Lengths of fur were thrown on many to be used to lie on or cover with on colder nights. Long tables were set along walls, which could be used for dining, although nobody actually sat at them to eat.

Leading off from this main hall were private chambers, usually three or four, more luxuriantly appointed than the public area. Here, there were well-shaped seats, more finely carved and polished, and large permanent sleeping pallets made of timber, cushioned with the softest furs.

Sarama led Sudas to the far end of the main hall as the rest of the pack followed, wagging tails, their eager barks ringing out loudly in the early morning air. His wife's retinue of personal women guards and maids were asleep on furs around the central fireplace and many stirred as he strode past, but did not rouse. They had done their share of carousing as well, singing, dancing and consuming their fill of soma; not with the menfolk as they might have preferred, but here in the privacy of their chamber. There were musical instruments laid on the tables, and he could only guess at the frolic and music that must have echoed in this hall only hours earlier. He did not regret denying them permission to bring their men into the hall to celebrate. The security of his queen and children outweighed their enjoyment.

Sarama pushed open the door to the queen's chamber behind the main hall, then trotted in happily, tail high in the air to indicate her pride in showing her master how well she had performed the task that was allotted to her. Sudas followed, amused at her enthusiasm. The usual two private chambers had been combined here to make one large apartment for his wife's use. In fact, the two chambers at the other end of the main hall were also connected to each other as well as to this large one, affording the queen of the Trtsus her privacy while permitting her staff to move freely behind doors.

It was impossible to make out who was sleeping beneath the luxuriant furs on the large bed. But Sarama's nose never failed her. She rummaged through the piles and sniffed out one errant little foot, another little palm and finally an adult female head covered with lustrous black hair as glossy as the Himalayan bear fur lying upon it. Having revealed the bed's occupants thus, she sat back and looked up at Sudas as if to say, 'See? Here they are, safe and sound as you left them.' Then she barked resonantly. Her pack had remained in the outer hall, knowing better than to broach the inner sanctum, but at the sound of Sarama's barking, the bolder ones sniffed at the door and thumped their tails against the log walls, wishing they could join in the play as usual.

Sudas got down on all fours and crawled on the bed. He found his son's little foot and tickled the bare sole with his fingers. The reaction was gratifying: The fur blanket rippled as little Indraut squirmed and squealed. He emerged protesting, face covered with his prominent fringe of hair. Sudas had already turned his attention to the bare palm exposed by Sarama. He tickled it and chuckled as his daughter Indrani reacted even more energetically than her older brother, her tousled head also emerging from the pile of furs.

Both children saw the culprit responsible for rousing them and attacked him with savage ferocity, tickling and squealing and jumping and yelling. Sarama encouraged them by barking loudly and thumping her tail hard against the head of the hapless remaining occupant of the bed. Sudas's queen Sudevi groaned and tried to look up, then covered her head at once as she saw the goings on around her.

Sudas collapsed in a paroxysm of laughter, pulling both his children to him. Sarama had to join in as well and she was included in the reconciliatory hug. For the next few moments, father, daughter, son and dog all lay on the pile of furs, locked in an affectionate embrace that was not dissimilar to some wrestling holds.

From beneath the tangled pile of furs, Sudevi's voice asked: 'Is the battle over? Is it safe to come out yet?'

5

THE LIGHT outside was glaucous, almost as if the hour were that of gloaming rather than daybreak. Sudas stood in the left courtyard before the entrance of the great hall and waited for his children. The great halls were all built with side and rear entrances only – front ingresses were prohibited by law. From where he stood, he could glimpse parts of other great halls, smoke curling steadily from their flues and adding to the misty haze of the early morning.

Apart from the buzz of activity in his own great hall, no other soul was astir at this hour. Even the dogs were asleep after the night of excitement and festivities. Beyond, the grama appeared quiet as well. The Trtsu tribe was a small one and nearly all its members had either been serving or being served in the wedding festivities of the past few days. They may not have had the finest soma or the choicest tidbits, but they had indulged sufficiently to need to sleep it off to recover. Sudas judged that it would be late morning before the grama's hustle and bustle resumed.

That was as close to a holiday as one got, when one was chief.

King, he reminded himself. *I'm to call myself King now, as is everyone else.* He shook his head at his own obduracy. *It just sounds so distanced, removed from everyone else. I'd much rather be just Sudas, son of Pijavana, son of Divodas of the line of Rishabha, son of Bharata, grama-chief of the Trtsu tribe. I'm no king, nor do I care about the politics of kingship.*

But he *was* the king and to those who followed him, the title mattered. It was easy enough for a king to self-deprecatingly shrug off his own title, but for his kshatriyas, his men at arms, it mattered whether they were serving a king, a chief, a grama-rakshak or a mere lord. Their fortunes and wealth rose and fell accordingly. For one thing, the number of kine a person received on being promoted to various positions differed. And kine, be it in the form of milch cows, bulls or even calves, was wealth, the only true wealth any person could possess in this world.

Apart from land, he reminded himself. Land was wealth too, under the new way of reckoning. But it would never be comparable to the wealth of cows and somehow, like his ancestors, he had never been able to fully embrace this modern concept of land belonging to any person, grama or clan. Land was mother earth, the womb and cradle of all life. How could any child claim exclusive ownership of a mother's embrace? She belonged to all who lived, human or otherwise. But the new laws proclaimed that land could be bought and sold and traded just like kine, and as chief – sorry, *king* – he had to respect the law and uphold it.

All thoughts of kingship dissipated at the sound of eager feet and happy voices. Sudevi emerged from the inner chamber, their son and daughter in tow, both flushed and excited at being able to accompany their father on this trip. They saw him waiting with the horses and broke out into a run, sandals thumping as they leaped, and skipped steps to race one another to the horses.

Sudevi stopped at the doorway, a fur wrapped around her shoulders, eyes still heavy with sleep. She rested her temple against the doorjamb, watching sleepily as the children reached their horses and began to clamber on. Sudas offered to hoist them up but they were outraged at the suggestion. They leaped up by themselves as he watched proudly. King he may be, but his children could ride and do everything that any Trtsu did, perhaps better than most. Not like the lazy overfed heirs of some grama-chiefs he had seen at the wedding festivities. A few even had little pot bellies protruding from their small frames, and required the assistance of liveried aides to climb upon their horses. He could not imagine any amount of wealth justifying such sloth. What did wealth have to do with it anyway? King or commoner, every man must lift his share of the burden and do his given chores. It was the only way a grama could survive and flourish.

But he reminded himself that all the tribes did not look at it the same way. Many of his neighbouring grama-chiefs and kings believed that the more cows one possessed, the less one needed to exert oneself. The logic behind this philosophy eluded him entirely. It went against the very grain of his own upbringing, which taught that every person or being was equal under dharma and must work ceaselessly at his own given tasks without thought of reward, rank or repercussion.

He glanced back at his wife and they exchanged a

glad smile and a sly look as he got onto his own horse.

It was an acknowledgement of the excitement their children were demonstrating, overjoyed at being treated to this special time with their pitr. Unlike the overfed grama-chiefs with pot-bellied sons, Sudas believed in matching his people burden for burden, strength for strength, as well as in setting an example for others to emulate. This meant that he often pulled more than his fair share, worked longer hours, and had less time to spare for himself and his filial obligations. It was also the reason why he had barely sipped a cup or two of soma the night before and all the nights of the festivities, and had stolen away from his rambunctious comrades to snatch a few hours of sleep in the privacy of the terrace of the empty southernmost great hall, reserved for sabha and samiti convocations. He had planned to be up early enough to be able to take his children on this trip and he was aware of the achievement of will and self-discipline it represented, as was his wife.

The look they gave each other was also a promise that after this excursion with the children, it would be their turn next. If the demands of kingship and grama-leadership were heavy, then the wedding festivities and the ongoing land law debates had added an elephant-load on Sudas's back. This had left him with much less time for his queen than they were accustomed to, and the two had indulged in far fewer intimacies than they mutually desired.

Sudevi's look had indicated that this lacuna would be rectified soon. For his part, he had responded with shining eyes that warned, *it had better be so!*

Now, he grinned again, turned the head of his horse and rode out of the courtyard of the great hall, his children whooping and following excitedly.

6

THE BOUNDARIES of Trtsu land were marked by rivers on three sides and mountains on the fourth. The rivers Parusni, Vipasha and Shatudri – also called Ravi, Beas and Satlej respectively by other tribes – roughly bordered the grama's western, southern and easternmost boundaries. Roughly, because the rivers were all sister waterways, often crisscrossing each other's paths, turning into tributaries of one another, disappearing into mountainous ground for sustained stretches, and changing their courses frequently. The river called Yamuna, for instance, was in fact a tributary of the greater river Saraswati. And many tribes considered Parusni to be a child of the river Saryu whereas the Trtsus called Saryu herself a child of Parusni. This was further compounded by the fact that Saryu was mainly a seasonal cascade and often disappeared altogether for years on end while Parusni, or Ravi, had been flowing strong for as long as humankind had resided in this region of Prithviloka. This fertile alluvial plain was known as the Land of Five Rivers. Of the plains nourished by the five rivers, the Trtsus occupied the most fertile portion of all. The location of their grama was perfect for defence as well as offence, bounded as it was by bodies of powerfully flowing waters on three fronts and the daunting Shivalik ranges to the northeast.

But the Trtsus had never considered the land to be exclusively theirs, certainly not in the limited sense that some gramas now used the concept of land-ownership. They regarded their occupancy as an allotted posting. Ever since the time of Yadu, forebear of the Yadava race, the Trtsus had been delegated the task of building a garrison here and ensuring that Mleccha invaders from the north and west did not maraud and raid at will. There were any number of Mleccha tribes that lived for nothing more than warring. They would ride down from the high plains of the far north, beyond the Himavat ranges, come down through the stony Pariyatra Parvata Pass, rampage across the rich lands of the Five Rivers, raiding, marauding, pillaging at will, and then return to boast of their spoils and encourage other Mlecchas to imitate their actions. With rifts and fissures expanding between the nations, and even between tribes and clans, these outposts were a crucial first line of defence against outside invasions.

If the Mleccha invaders were not checked early, the beautiful lush northern plains fed by the five great watercourses would have been relegated to little more than a hunting ground overrun by plunderers and pillagers. It was the Trtsus who guarded this beautiful land and for this purpose had made it their home; where else would a sentry stand but on the border of the land he protected? So the Trtsus kept a perpetual watch at this strategic location, guarding the way to the great subcontinent, a treasure trove of the greatest natural resources, Vedanta (spiritual knowledge) and geographical beauty. Indeed, it was not just the northern plains they protected, but the entire subcontinent that lay beyond it. It extended from the great kingdoms of the southern peninsula, where their sibling tribes had developed their own unique cultural identity, including their own dialect of Sanskrit, all the way across to the far eastern lands and the illustrious civilisations of the Chin peoples and beyond. The Pariyatra Parvata Pass was a gateway to the entire civilised world in this age, and the subcontinent one of the choicest jewels in the crown.

Although the Shivalik Mountains were on the northern and northwestern edges of Trtsu land, there was one substantial peak on the southeastern boundary as well, within sight of the Vipasha River. This great rise qualified as a mountain only by a few score yards, but due to the relative flatness of its immediate surroundings, it towered above the countryside like a giant standing among sleeping dwarves. It was a solitary exception to its northern brethren, isolated over the ages by the profusion of rivers flowing through these plains, a magnificent peak with gently rising grassy slopes that sometimes attracted a little snowfall in the deepest winter. The snowfall and the runoff each subsequent spring had left the summit stone-bare, which lent it the air of a balding patriarch in the lush post-monsoon autumn.

The Trtsus had nicknamed it Uttunga, The Tall One.

It was to Uttunga that Sudas rode with his children this morning. It was a special treat the children got only on rare occasions. They loved the ride as well as the climb. Due to the gentle rise of its slopes and a well-worn spiralling pathway, their horses could take them most of the way up. The last few hundred yards they climbed were hard but not impossible for nine-year-old Indrani and eleven-year-old Indraut. Brother and sister vied with each other to show their pitr how well they could climb, even when both had sweat pouring down their faces despite the crisp cool air at this height. When they finally broke through the grassy skirt and stumbled with obvious relief onto the stony crown, both turned at once to each other and yelled, 'I was first!'

Sudas put his arms around their shoulders, helping support them as he continued moving upwards. 'You were both first.'

They looked at one another.

'You did climb well even though you are younger than me,' Indraut said to his sister imperiously.

Indrani shrugged. 'You climbed quite well for a boy,' she replied.

Indraut bristled. 'I am *not*—' he began, but Sudas intervened, cutting him off quickly. 'She means for a male. She knows you're not a boy anymore, but a man now, do you not, Indrani?'

Indrani looked at her brother speculatively. Indraut's eyes narrowed. She smiled disarmingly. 'Yes, that is what I meant, Pitr. He climbs well for a man.'

Indraut, keying himself up for a sibling spat, blinked and grinned suddenly, disarmed. 'It was a tie,' he conceded generously.

Indrani nodded. 'Close enough.' She tossed her thick long braid over her shoulder and turned to look up at the last few yards of the climb that were left. 'Shall we race to the top now? I warrant I can reach before—'

'No racing,' Sudas said quickly. 'We musn't disturb Guru Vashishta's tapasya.'

Both nodded in exactly the same solemn way, imitating Sudevi perfectly. He smiled and tousled their heads affectionately. Ah, it was wonderful to have children.

They were about to move on when he felt a sudden warmth on the back of his hand. He turned and saw the fog on the northeastern mountain ranges dissipating to allow the rising sun to shine through.

'Wait, let us rest a moment and allow Surya Deva to warm us first.'

They sat on a shelf of rock, worn perfectly smooth by millennia of rain and snowmelt. The sun had risen almost two hours earlier but due to the veil of haze in the east, had not actually broken through. It was a pleasure to see it appear, just over the top of the snowcapped Shivalik range, an orange ball of fire whose warmth lit his body. He looked down at his son and daughter, seated on either side of him, at their upturned faces lit by the pure clean light, clean straight features so much like his wife's, and felt that today would be a good day. Any day when one had so much love to hold on to was a very good day.

He glanced back over his shoulder and saw that stormy clouds were moving in from the southwest. It looked like it might rain today, perhaps a heavy shower. So be it. Indra, Lord of Thunder, Lightning and Rain, was a hallowed ancestor and patron deity, and if he chose to scold and bathe the Trtsus, such was his right.

Besides, the additional rain would be good for the rivers, and the waterworks they were building also depended on a vigorous torrent. The more the better. It was all Indra's blessings in the end.

It would be a very good day no matter what. He found nothing that could dissuade him of that belief.

7

GURU VASHISHTA was not alone. Sudas and his children were still a score yards from the crest when they heard the voices – one gruff and raised in anger, the other quiet and moderated. The wind at the summit whipped away most sounds, so the fact that they could hear any voice at all indicated the intensity of emotions being exchanged.

Both Indrani and Indraut looked up repeatedly at the summit and exchanged curious glances, but neither asked their father any questions. They were old enough to have heard arguments between men before, especially between these two men.

The apex of Uttunga was not dissimilar to the bald crown atop an aging man's head. The rock shelving, worn down by the accumulation of water and snowmelt, sank into a gentle depression at the peak.

This was the result of perhaps a million winters. Sudas and his children reached this demi-plateau of craggy stone, and climbed over the sloping rim to step onto a nearly flat plate of smooth stone. The sides of the plate gently sloped inwards, just enough for water to collect at its centre, but not so sharp a gradient that it hampered walking. It was an ideal site to build a fortress, had the Trtsus wished it. And he knew his forebears had considered the matter several times over the decades.

But what would be the point? Uttunga's best view was of the southernmost parts of Trtsu territory, the area where the civilised lands of the subcontinent, populated by friendly tribes, lay. Those that were not friendly were not hostile either, merely neutral or distanced. No threat was going to come from the south or even southeast or southwest.

The only real danger lay northwards and westwards. Thence came the Mlecchas, barbaric invaders from foreign lands. Had Uttunga been at the northernmost extent of Trtsu territories, his father or his forefathers would have definitely considered undertaking the effort needed to build a fortress upon this summit. But in its present location, it would be relegated to a pleasure palace, and the Trtsus did not indulge in selfish pleasures. They were rakshaks, given the task of guarding the tribes, clans and assorted villages and allies of their homeland against foreign invasion, not rich indolents who could waste away their days in idle sloth.

So it had been declared a long time ago that the peak of Uttunga would be given over to Indra. The simple stone structure that stood in the centre of the depression, atop the summit of Uttunga, was symbolic of the diety.

It was towards this structure that he now walked with his son and daughter.

Lord Indra was the patron deity of the Trtsu Bharatas. Any place dedicated to him was left exposed to the elements, rather than being enclosed or sheltered from his gifts of rain, lightning, wind and thunder. The structure on Uttunga was a simple stone slab carved from the granite shelf of the mountain itself, as bare as an altar of sacrifice, with only a central yagna chaukat to contain Agni and a few tall rods to carry the krtadhvaj of the clan.

This was the Cradle of Agni.

It was in this sacred spot that the preceptor of

the Trtsu tribe and the Bharata race in general kept the sacred fire fed.

Brahmarishi Vashishta, patron guru to Sudas's family and tribe, his closest advisor and guide, mentor to his ancestors and his children and overseer of all major rituals and sacrifices also spent his spare time here, meditating in wind-blown solitude. At this hour, on this particular day, Sudas had expected to find the guru alone, cross-legged in Indra's place, meditating or perhaps contemplating the momentous transition that the Trtsus were about to make.

But as they had already heard, Guru Vashishta was not alone. Nor was he meditating.

There were two brahmins, not one, in red ochre garb in the sacred space of Indra. Both were tall, one as tall as Sudas himself, the other a whole head taller and formidable in form, as befitted a former raj-kshatriya turned brahmin. The taller man was Brahmarishi Vishwamitra and the sight of him did not please Sudas. He would not have brought his children here today had he known Vishwamitra would be present.

Vishwamitra's was the louder voice they had heard while approaching. As it usually was. The former warrior-king had a dominating personality and was accustomed to having his way in all matters. As a king he had waged war almost incessantly, to the point where his enemies had begun to join forces against him in a desperate bid to thwart his insatiable ambition. Even after he had renounced his kingdom and taken to a life of meditation, he had carried the same warlike approach into the pursuit of spiritual goals. It had been said that even Almighty Brahma hesitated to deny Vishwamitra any wish, for fear that the brahmarishi might curse him. His reputation preceded him, and every king, chieftain or kshatriya across the world awaited the day when Vishwamitra might appear on his threshold, demanding guru-dakshina, the undeniable debt that every member of the warrior varna owed to those of the brahmin varna. It was the debt of shishya to guru or student to teacher, and could not be denied, even if granting the wish bankrupted, ruined or ended the life of the kshatriya in question.

But if there was one person who owed no debt to Vishwamitra, nor feared or was intimidated by his formidable will and reputation, it was Brahmarishi Vashishta. In fact, if there was one person who had stood up to Vishwamitra, resisting his will and refusing to give in to his demands, it was his senior saptarishi.

The two great brahmins had a long history of conflict, and it was partly this conflict that had caused Sudas's forefathers to choose to honour Vashishta as their official preceptor even though Vishwamitra remained official preceptor to all the Bharata tribes.

As Sudas looked at the angry face of Vishwamitra and the manner in which he confronted Vashishta on Mount Uttunga, he thought it seemed certain that the old rivalry would break into a fresh round of hostilities.

8

'Reconsider, wise one,' Vishwamitra was saying. 'I appeal to your good sense one more time.' The hard lines and edges on the brahmarishi's face and the ferocity of his voice reflected the man's warrior-like approach to his brahminical calling.

Sudas had stopped with his children at the edge of the Cradle. The wind at the top of Uttunga was violent and tore away spoken words the moment they were out of one's mouth. But even so, Vishwamitra's voice carried clearly to him and he wished his son and daughter did not have to witness this unfortunate moment.

Guru Vashishta replied with the serene yogic calm for which he was renowned, 'The Trtsu Bharatas are righteous under dharma. As their guru, I shall support them no matter what opposition they may face. Such is *my* dharma.'

Vishwamitra's beard bristled. It was the wind that shook the flowing white locks but the impression given was one of intense rage, barely withheld. It was an impression that was justified, given the brahmarishi's notorious temper. Even as he continued speaking, the fury in his eyes and quivering voice were matched by his ominous baritone,

'You walk a dangerous path, Vashishta. A lonely and treacherous way, and if you persist you shall swiftly lead the Trtsus into the bed of the river where their bones shall lie until picked clean by river turtles and bleached by the rushing waters, uncremated and unmourned.'

Vashishta turned his head a fraction, allowing himself to gaze northwards, towards the Trtsu city, unperturbed by Vishwamitra's intensity or warning.

'Death comes to us all in the end, Vishwamitra. As my former pupil you know this well. I have taught you the Tataka mantra and told you its significance. One day we must all cross the river. Whether we reach the far side or are taken by the waters, hardly matters. Cremated, buried, hung in trees, thrown into dry wells, torn to pieces, eaten by wolves… the manner in which Yama takes our corporeal bodies may differ, but the end is always the same. Better to live the little time we have left by performing the tasks we are given to the best of our abilities, regardless of the odds or the consequences. Better to die fighting for what we believe in than live long by corrupting our own ideals and convictions. For a victory that is gained by the defeat of our own principles remains hollow!'

Vishwamitra made a sound almost like that of an enraged animal, such that Sudas almost started forward, thinking the younger brahmarishi was about to attack the elder one. He stopped himself in time as he realised the sound was merely one of disgust.

'Vashishta, your transcendental yogic insights are useless in this context. This is not a battle of principles, values or your precious dharma! It is a very real and practical war of conflicting goals. Either you use your influence with the Trtsus to persuade them to walk the path of reason or you lead them to their doom. I have had my fill of your pearls of wisdom. Answer me now: Will you or will you not do your task as guru to the Trtsus and advise them to see sense in this matter?'

Vashishta smiled. 'I am doing my task. The Trtsus are the only ones who see the sense in this matter. Sudas is no fool, to betray the pact his forebears made, just because you will it so. He will adhere to his dharma, and certainly not yield to my persuasions to do otherwise. The task you thrust upon me is not mine to execute.'

Vishwamitra glared down at Vashishta. 'Yet you have great influence over him. He will heed your advice. He will listen to your wisdom. You are his guru!'

'And as his guru, I must only give him advice that is in his best interest. What you ask me to say is not wisdom, it is madness.'

'Is it madness to want to survive, as a man, a family, a tribe? Is it madness to refuse great riches, wealth and increased power? Is it madness to do what one must in order to survive in the face of insurmountable odds?'

For the first time since they had come within hearing range of the two duelling brahmarishis, Sudas heard Vishwamitra's tone soften and grow gentler. There was genuine caring in it now, the respectful tone that befitted a younger brahmin when addressing his senior – his own guru, as it were – and Sudas was heartened to hear it. Perhaps a resolution was about to be attained after all.

'Vashishta,' Vishwamitra went on in this new, gentler tone, 'I beseech you. Surely you see that the true madness lies in not listening to my warning. In ignoring the reality of the situation. In failing to compromise and concede defeat gracefully. In risking the ruin of all he holds dear and the genocide of his entire tribe and lineage. Even now there is time. Speak to Sudas. Make him see reason. The world is changing. The old ways are gone and fast growing irrelevant. The age of dharma is long past. This is the dawn of the age of wealth and power. The age of war. A man must be strong to survive it. A chieftain must do what is best for his people. A king must act wisely and deal felicitously. The circumstances call for introspection and change.'

Vishwamitra turned on his heel and took several strides, creating distance between himself and his interlocutor. He stopped at the edge of the Cradle, then spread his hands wide, holding out the great longstaff he carried to extend his already prodigious reach to encompass the breadth and width of the entire Five Rivers kingdom. He made a powerful imposing figure. The wind rose in intensity, adding its piercing shriek to the ominous power of his speech.

'The Age of Kali is nigh. In this coming age, only those who understand the language of iron shall survive and thrive. Iron has no dharma. Iron cuts through flesh and shatters bone. And without flesh and bone, even a dream of dharma cannot be sustained, let alone the thing itself. Times are changing. This great land of the Five Rivers is a rich and fertile treasure trove waiting to be plundered by men of iron. Those who ally with them will reap their share of riches. Those who oppose them foolishly will be sundered by it. They shall be kings who bear these swords of untold power; they shall be emperors of the earth and all within it. All they desire shall be within their grasp and none may dare deny them.'

He turned and pointed the end of his staff at Vashishta. 'Will you stand with us or against us?'

9

VASHISHTA HAD stood as he was, neither turning to follow Vishwamitra with his eyes nor his head. Then, he turned his face to the other brahmarishi and Sudas was startled to see a smile upon that ancient face. It was a gentle, almost mischievous smile, such as he might have expected to see on Indrani or Indraut's face. To see it on the wizened lined features of an illustrious preceptor such as Guru Vashishta was not only a surprise, but also curiously pleasing and reassuring. Something about that smile and the guileless ease with which it faced the stormy bluster of the other brahmarishi was greatly encouraging. Slowly, the smile faded, and gave way to a sadder, wiser expression, tinged with an undertone of something ominous, something even more formidable than Vishwamitra's haranguing.

'Those who divide the world into factions for and

against...' began Vashishta in a voice that was as quiet as always, yet no less audible despite the raging wind atop the summit. Sudas could not make out how this could be, for Vishwamitra had been battling the same raging wind by almost shouting at the top of his voice. Yet, Vashishta appeared to be speaking normally, as if he were in a quiet stone temple rather than on a gale-swept mountaintop. Sudas could hear every word as clear as the ringing of a temple bell on a still day.

Vashishta rephrased his statement in an attempt at being conciliatory: 'Those who split the world into us and them, you and me, Trtsus and Bharatas, Aryas and Mlecchas, darker and lighter, stronger and weaker, dharma and adharma, richer and poorer, older and younger, brahmin and kshatriya, male and female, two-legged and four-legged, right-handed and left-handed, carapaced and skin-covered... those who are stupid enough to think that all of us who ride upon this great grama of a world, huddled together inside the wagon-womb of Prithvi-Maa, are separate and not dependent one upon the other for *all* our survival, those who believe that fighting one another is necessary, even desirable, and fail to see that we are only fighting ourselves, fail to realise that the resources we fight over are already ours to share, to use, to conserve and renew. They fail to see that by waging war against one another we only risk setting fire to and damaging our own grama, the one great wagon in which we all ride together, fellow-journeyers in the endless caravan of existence. Those who brand their kine with a mark as if a symbol burned into the skin of a cow makes it your cow and not your brother's cow, those who issue ultimatums of With or Against…' pausing now and raising his own hands in a clear imitation of Vishwamitra's actions, 'you who subscribe to such delusions already stand against your own self. Your war is with your own inner madness. Your battle is with your own stubborn will. Your conflict is with the demon that you have created and named your enemy, yet it is nothing more than your own obverse reflection. You fight because you wish to fight. You take up the sword of iron because you love iron and because you love to sunder flesh and bone. It does not matter why. It does not matter where or when or to whom. All that matters to you is the lust for battle and the lust for power. And a hatred of those who stand alone and refuse to let you have your way. Go then, go gather your men of iron. Go whip them into a frenzy. Go prepare your white hot cattle brands. These threats are as the wind to the lion's mane. You will ruffle his fur but you cannot bear him down. In the end, the world will change but the one who remains upon it will be he who cherishes the gift of life and sustenance given by this earth we reside on, and cares for it as a gardener cares for his patch. Swords will rust, axes will grow dull, but the earth shall endure, and those who embrace it with love shall endure as well. Go from this place, *vish*-tongued Vishwamitra! Take your poisonous words with you! The Trtsus reside here, on the land of their ancestors and the stronghold of dharma, in the shelter of Indra and Varuna. They shall reside for a thousand years. Neither you nor your iron-tongued conspirators shall unseat them. I, Vashishta, proclaim it so.'

Vishwamitra glared at the senior brahmarishi and the two great sages stood thus, gazes locked with a resoluteness that seemed capable of lasting for all infinity. Neither budged nor blinked.

Then with a suddenness and strength that belied his age and varna, Vishwamitra raised his staff and brought it down hard on the stone floor of the Cradle. The stone cracked. Sudas saw the ripples spread like a spider web outward from the point of impact, and when the brahmarishi raised the staff again, he saw the nub-hole in the stone made by the end of his staff. Even though it was made of lohitstone, the famed ironwood of the northern regions, how strong could the staff be to crack solid stone? And how strong was the brahmarishi himself?

Sudas had kept his hands on the shoulders of his children all this while, to restrain them should they get the urge to run across the Cradle to the guru, as well as to reassure them with his touch and presence. He had felt their tension as the debate raged on. It was never a happy sight to see two adults arguing, but to see two gurus, preceptors of their faith and tribe, the most exalted and wise minds of their kind, was unsettling in the extreme. Sudas himself felt shaken by the debate he had witnessed, even though he did not know what it meant or what they had been arguing about. He had some notion though; the rivalry between Vishwamitra and Vashishta was an old one, dating back to the time since before he was born. And he possessed an understanding of the complex web of politics and powerplay that the two sages represented, so this was not completely surprising. But to his children, raised to respect great learning and sage wisdom above all else and to address a guru as 'deva', for a teacher was no less than a god to them, the argument had been very disturbing. He felt it now in the way their bodies shook, with barely suppressed anger and emotion. He squeezed their shoulders reassuringly, but knew that nothing could mitigate the shock of seeing their two most venerated elders attack each other so furiously, almost coming to blows, and then, to see Vishwamitra strike at the Cradle of Agni, the most sacred site of their tribe, and desecrate it thus.

As Vishwamitra came towards them in order to descend the rough track that led down the side of the mountain, Sudas felt Indraut break free of his grasp and run to bar the sage's path.

10

'GURUDEV!' CRIED Indraut, clearly impassioned by what he had seen and heard. 'Why do you do this? We are your people, you are our guru. You are supposed to guide and protect us! Please, do not go away in anger.'

Vishwamitra stared down at the young boy barring his way. His face was filled with an emotion unlike anything Sudas could name or decipher. It was something beyond rage, the distant hundred-yojana stare of a warrior in the cold grip of battle madness. The staff in his hand seemed as deadly as any sword or spear. And even a thousand heads of armoured horsemen behind him could not have made him seem more formidable and threatening.

Without a word, he strode forward, bearing down on little Indraut.

The sight reminded Sudas of a rhinoceros charging

at a young buck, except that any young buck would have bolted at once, running for his life.

But Indraut stood his ground.

'Gurudev!' cried the young boy plaintively, clearly beseeching, not threatening – as if an unarmed eleven-year-old boy could be threatening to a powerful raj-kshatriya turned brahmarishi like Vishwamitra.

Still Vishwamitra strode directly at Indraut, as if meaning to knock him down and topple him off the side of the summit.

Little Indrani left Sudas's grip and sprang forward at once, going to her brother's aid. 'Gurudev!' she exclaimed, adding to her brother's plea.

Sudas moved faster, swooping down and snatching his son out of the way. He swung him around, just as Vishwamitra strode past the spot that Indraut had occupied only a fraction of a moment earlier. Putting him down gently on his feet again, he turned to see the back of the brahmarishi disappear as he stepped down from the Cradle of Agni and was gone from sight. He caught Indrani's little wrist as well and brought her closer. She embraced her brother tightly.

'Indraut, I thought he was going to kill you!' she cried.

Both brother and sister sat down on the stone Cradle, comforting one another.

Assured that they were safe, Sudas turned to look at brahmarishi Vashishta.

Vashishta was staring in the direction Vishwamitra had gone. There was an expression of infinite sadness on his careworn face. It was an expression Sudas had not seen often on that ancient face. Most of the lines on Vashishta's face were lines of amusement and laughter rather than sadness.

'Gurudev,' he said quietly, greeting his preceptor with the appropriate gestures and tone. 'What was the purpose of Guru Vishwamitra's visit here? What did you two debate about so fiercely? He appeared to be asking you to warn me in particular about something. What is that thing and why was it so urgent and critical?'

Vashishta sighed and sat cross-legged on the stone floor of the Cradle, near the spot where Vishwamitra had struck his staff. 'He was asking me to tell you not to begin the reconstruction.'

Sudas was taken aback. Of all the things he had thought of during the moments he had observed the debate between the two gurus, this was the last thing he had expected to hear. 'The reconstruction of the city?'

'Yes,' Vashishta said. 'You are to begin tomorrow at daybreak, for that is the auspicious hour that I prescribed for the commencement of the work. He wished me to prevail upon you not to begin as planned.'

'I do not understand,' Sudas said.

And he truly did not.

The Trtsus had been planning to rebuild their city at a site near their present location, using a city plan that had been developed over decades. It envisaged a city utilising the greatest advancements in architecture, town planning, road building, house construction, and sewage disposal. In short, it would be the most modern city ever designed and built by the human mind and hand. While timber structures were warm and comfortable and familiar, they were susceptible to destruction by fire – a substantive hazard for people who kept the sacred Agni perpetually burning in the centre of their homes – apart from being prone to other limitations.

The new plan called for double-storeyed buildings of fired brick based on a new design, using a new combination of mud, water and straw baked in special kilns that produced bricks which could build walls capable of withstanding almost anything short of a direct charge by an armoured elephant. There would be avenues ten yards wide, lying perfectly perpendicular to one another and running precisely north to south, east to west. There would be underground drains connected to every house – each of which would have its own privy – that carried away all sewage from the city to a suitable spot where it would be used to produce organic gases that could be trapped and used for other purposes, with the remaining effluent burned off or turned into compost fertiliser, rather than simply dumped into the rivers as most tribes did now. Common bathing houses would enable the citizens to bathe regularly in a socially inviting environment that would foster inter-varna and even inter-tribe interaction on a daily basis.

Unlike some tribes, the Trtsus had no inhibitions about interaction between varnas and considered all people equal, regardless of whether they were brahmins engaged in rote learning, warriors who killed and fought for a living, merchants who travelled and traded and dealt in coin or those who performed the most menial tasks. The new sewage system alone would revolutionise everyday life – each householder would be able to clean their own privy, and the city employees would deal with sewage transport, conversion and disposal. There would be no need to have separate sub-varnas delegated solely to the task of cleaning privies and drains.

'Gurudev,' said Sudas, now genuinely baffled. 'The new city design and plan is revolutionary, we know this. But why does it trouble Brahmarishi Vishwamitra of all people? How can our plans to reform and reconstruct the city possibly anger him?' He added as an afterthought: 'Is it the democratisation of the varnas that he objects to?'

Vashishta was running the palm of his hand over the spider web of cracks. He traced them to their origin, then probed the nub-hole with his finger, pushing down. Sudas could see the guru's long bony finger disappear beyond the first joint. 'It is not that, nor is it civic planning that troubles him. It is the city itself.'

Sudas still could not understand. 'But why? This is a plan that has been developed since my grandfather's time. I am only implementing it now. It has been debated and discussed and vetted a hundred times, as it is a matter concerning the whole tribe. It has passed debates and subsequent voting in the samiti and the sabha before finally coming to the king for his seal of approval.'

Vashishta held out a hand. 'Give me your knife, if you will, Sudas.'

Sudas complied, slipping out the stabbing knife from the sheath on his belt and handing it grip-first to the preceptor. 'You know whereof I speak. It is not some kingly whim that I dreamed up one morning!'

Vashishta smiled. 'You speak truly, Sudas. The Trtsu lords and ladies are not given over to selfish whims. You are the epitome of dharma, one and all.'

Sudas was not sure whether every single Trtsu of his line had been utterly above reproach, just as he did not think of himself as the divine lord of dharma that he was sometimes made out to be in hymns and invocations, but that was beside the point. He persisted, 'Then what is it about the city plan that offends Guru Vishwamitra so?'

Vashishta probed the hole with the point of the knife, bringing up crumbled rock powder and marble-sized pieces. He excavated the hole as he replied, 'It is a fortress, Sudas. You know that, just as well as your forefathers did. A fortress of stone and brick, impenetrable to arrows, spears, darts, and most weaponry. Once garrisoned within, your people could hold the city for months. The network of tunnels for maintenance of the sewage system as well as to allow for river flooding, the underground granaries, the intricate architectural genius of the whole design, the very sturdiness of the new-fired bricks that shall be used in its construction, makes for the most formidable defence known to civilised man in this day and age. Once it is built and supplied with stores, the Trtsus will be invulnerable to siege or attack.'

Sudas nodded slowly. 'Yes, I do see the military advantage it will give us. But how does that affect anyone else? It is a defencive system, not an offencive one. We can hardly cart bricks or tunnels or sewage systems and use them to attack our neighbours! Besides, the Trtsu garrison has been stationed in this confluence of the Five Rivers for more time than I can recall. Whether we man the garrison with timber palaces or brick houses, what does it matter to anyone except our arch enemies?'

'It is your enemies who are objecting, Sudas. It is they who do not wish you to build a fortress for your garrison. For once you do, they will lose their opportunity to strike at you. Which is why they must now do so before your city is built. While you are still vulnerable and naked.'

Vashishta raised the knife in his hand and stabbed it into the hole in the Cradle. It sank to the hilt.

11

'Pitr!'

Indraut's voice cut through Sudas's thoughts. He looked up to see both his son and daughter standing at the edge of the Cradle, looking southwards. The pathway leading up was on the south face of Uttunga, so his first thought was that they were looking at Vishwamitra descending. But they were looking farther outward, in the direction of the river.

He started to call back, then realised the wind was blowing away from him; instead, he raised a hand, palm outwards, indicating to them to wait. Indrani nodded and whispered something in her brother's ear. Sudas saw Indraut nod curtly, his little chin set firmly in a grim expression and was struck by how much they both resembled him in attitude and behaviour, even as they resembled their maatr physically.

He turned his attention back to Guru Vashishta. The aged preceptor was digging. Sudas looked down at the hole the old brahmarishi had enlarged with his knife. Apparently, the rift caused by Vishwamitra's blow had been powerful enough to create a deep crack in the stone slab. He saw powdery rubble disappear inwards as Vashishta stabbed downwards with the blade. Sudas winced at the use being made of his fine blade. He sharpened that knife himself, as he did all his blades. A good kshatriya cared personally for his weapons and his mounts.

'Gurudev,' he said, unable to understand the concentration and energy the preceptor was lavishing on the strange task. 'You believe that we will be attacked before we can finish constructing the new city? That is what Vishwamitra threatened?'

Vashishta paused in his digging to brush away a lock of hair that had fallen across his face. He looked up at Sudas with half his face concealed by long white hair, the other side held up by the hand holding the knife. Sudas could not help but notice that the blade was already looking duller and blunted by the misuse, but said nothing.

'Do not concern yourself with Vishwamitra's

threats,' Vashishta said. His hair swirled about his face in the rising wind. 'It is the forces he speaks for that should concern you. For all his faults, Vishwamitra is still a brahmarishi and a Vedic master. Those whom he advises, however, are nothing more than avaricious beasts. They will sooner destroy you than parley. Vishwamitra sought to avoid a calamity, not to threaten to cause it.'

Sudas shook his head doubtfully. 'Yet he said things I would not have permitted any man to say to my guru. Nor would you have permitted him either, had you not had your reasons.'

Vashishta looked at Sudas for a moment, holding his gaze. Slowly, a smile lit his thin lips, although the warmth from the smile never reached his eyes. 'You are the wisest and best of all my pupils, Sudas. I have great hopes for you. Remember that calamities will come, be it today or the next day. It is how we weather them that defines us. A crisis is a turning point in both the best and worst senses of the term. The wise man turns even the gravest crisis to his advantage. It is at the moment of greatest danger that a man has the opportunity to display his greatest strengths.'

Sudas was still contemplating that choice portion

of wisdom when he heard the voices of his children calling again.

Vashishta nodded in their direction without looking. 'Go, attend to your heirs. They are the future of the Trtsus and of the Bharata nation.'

Sudas wanted to say more, to hear more.

He knew that once this moment passed, he would never be able to speak to the guru in this specific context. Vashishta was not one for spelling things out. He liked his students to be independent-minded and able to reason for themselves, often only intervening to cryptically bless them or express disappointment at their conclusions. It could be frustrating when one was young and impatient, but as Sudas had aged and matured, he had realised the guru had taught him the greatest lesson of all – to be independent of one's own teacher.

Now, as Vashishta turned his attention back to the singularly odd task of digging a hole in the stone surface of the summit, Sudas knew that this particular lesson had ended. He would have to figure the rest out for himself. To ask more pointed or pertinent questions would be to insult his guru's estimation of himself.

He rose to his feet and walked over to the edge.

The wind was stronger, buffetting him so hard that he had to keep his feet wide apart. He frowned, wondering if Indrani and Indraut could stand up to it, but from the looks of it, they seemed to be doing fine. He guessed that their shorter height and the way they crouched helped to diminish the force of the wind. That, and the fact that they were standing near the windward edge reassured him only a little – the wind was holding them back off the edge, rather than pushing them towards it. Even so, his fatherly heart could not rest easy with them so close to danger. If the wind were to change suddenly, or Vishwamitra return for some reason…

'Move back from the edge, both of you,' he said as he approached.

They did so at once. Indrani caught his arm and held on to it. Sudas saw her anxious face. She had been shaken by the argument between the gurus but had recovered quickly. After all, she was a Trtsu. War and conflict were but a part of their daily duty.

Yes, but one's gurus are not supposed to turn on their child pupils. That old brahmin would have knocked both Indraut and Indrani off the mountain had I not moved them aside in time.

'What is it, son?' he asked Indraut who had cupped his hand over his eyes to protect them from the furious wind. There was no need to guard against sunlight as the cloudy dawn had given way to a gloomy morning. Patches of sunlight shone through gaps in a steadily accumulating carpet of clouds.

Indraut responded by pointing.

Sudas looked. He felt Indrani's hand tighten on his forearm as she followed his gaze and knew that whatever they had seen was troubling.

12

Sudas spotted the movement easily. The tributary of the Parusni river was a few miles south of Uttunga and marked the border of Trtsu territory. On either side of the river were vast empty fields of kusa grass, lush and green from the monsoon rains. Patches of sunlight striking at a slanting angle through the clouds fell upon portions of this vast field, turning it into a quilted pattern of light and dark green grass that rippled and undulated like the ocean. Against this vast ocean of light and green kusa stalks, a darker silhouette was moving at galloping speed. Seen from this height and distance, it was barely the size of a flea, but Sudas knew at once what that tiny speck was, as it crept steadily across the great grassy expanse.

It was a rider, coming from the river, heading into Trtsu lands.

He was coming fast, riding all out like a man fleeing for his life.

Sudas felt Indrani pull at his arm. She pointed silently, indicating a point about a mile beyond the rider, closer to the river.

Sudas looked.

And saw a whole group of gnats, bunched together, coming from the river. At this distance, they crept across the sea of grass too, but he knew that on the ground they were actually a group of riders, racing at full gallop.

Riders.

A dozen and a half. Perhaps a full score.

He also saw the brown rectangular man-made object on the river just beyond them.

A raft, pulled by ropes. At the narrowest point of the tributary, the one place where no river crossing is permitted, by Trtsu law. That is why we have outriders posted at that point, to watch against possible intruders.

The outriders had never needed to ride back to report trouble, since the land across the river was friendly land. Bharata land in fact.

Now that he knew what he was looking at, he crouched down, cupping his own hands over his eyes, and scoured the area around the river meticulously, as quickly as he could.

The far side of the river at that point was covered by a thicket, blocking his view, so he could not see if there were more riders on the other bank. But he sensed a stir of darker shadows within the thicket which might suggest that there were men camped there, waiting for the raft to return so they could cross and follow the leaders.

Speaking of which, the riders on the Trtsu side were distinct enough. They were clearly chasing the lone rider who, Sudas suspected, was none other than one of his own outriders posted at that crossing.

Which means they are hostile, why else would they be chasing my outrider?

Indrani tugged at his arm.

He looked at her. From his present squatting position, he was on the same eye level as she was. She looked into his face with large deep brown eyes crinkling at the corners in a striking imitation of her mother's familiar frown.

'Who is it, Pitr? Who are those riders?' Even her voice echoed her mother's voice in pitch and accent.

Trouble, he thought to himself. *Trouble of the kind*

Guru Vishwamitra was threatening. Mischief-makers trying to send a message to me to underline what the guru tried to convey through words, or perhaps worse.

Aloud he said, 'I do not know, Indrani, but I intend to find out. Indraut?' He stood up.

Both his son and daughter looked up at him expectantly, their faces flushed, their eyes bright and alert.

Sudas glanced over at the centre of the Cradle. Guru Vashishta was still digging with the knife, doing something that was apparently important to him. Sudas did not have time to waste finding out what the guru was up to. His crisis, it seemed, had already begun.

He turned his attention back to his children, speaking softly and carefully, using the age-old trick of speaking *under* the wind rather than trying to shout over it. As a wise man had once taught him: *You cannot fight the gods of weather and nature. You can only trick them sometimes!*

He told his children: 'I want both of you to listen to me very carefully and do exactly as I say.'

They listened.

Moments later, he was racing down the mountainside. He moved at a speed that would have been impossible for his son and daughter to match, or dangerous if they attempted it. Their young bodies were not developed enough to do something like this. As it was, he came dangerously close to losing control and falling down to certain death. It was only his years of experience with such dangerous sport that kept him moving downwards rather than simply tumbling head over heels. His mother had been from the high mountains and her people were accustomed to living on the side of high precipices. In her village, even little children played and frolicked on narrow ledges and ponies could gallop up and down mountainsides. Sudas had benefitted from her experiences as she had taught him everything she knew, starting with the ability to treat the side of even the highest mountain as simply another walking surface. 'The only difference,' she had said, 'is that the world is a little more tilted than it usually is. You just need to compensate for it, without thinking about it.'

Now, he used every skill she had taught him, as well as the experience gained from the times he and his maternal cousins had raced and played up and down the sides of mountains – including this very peak. He had done this very thing, racing down Uttunga's side, any number of times. The only catch was, the last time he had done it was over a decade ago, before Indraut had been born. Still, he found the technique coming back to him instinctively. Even if his mind had forgotten some of the lessons, his body remembered all.

The horses whinnied in surprise when he reached the base of the mountain several moments later, and he could understand why. They were not accustomed to their master leaping down mountains to land in their midst, dusty and grass-covered. He had no time to soothe and reassure them but clicked his customary greeting and they subsided at once, pushing their long snouts at him to confirm that it was indeed their master.

He untied Saryu with dexterity, leaped onto her back and broke her into a canter. He was half way up the mountain's skirting side, but the pathway was rock, washed clean of mud by the last rains, and Saryu had sure footing.

'Ride, my beauty,' he whispered in her ear. 'We must reach that outrider before his pursuers do.'

13

COMING DOWN the gently sloping side of Mount Uttunga, Sudas had an excellent view of the situation. The outrider was about a mile away, moving at an angle that would take him past Uttunga and towards the city. Sudas could cut him off there, at that pile of rocks.

But the pursuers had gained considerably on their quarry. When Sudas had glimpsed them from the summit, they had probably just landed on the riverbank and had not yet worked up to their full speed. Besides, horses always ran faster in packs than alone. He estimated grimly that they too would catch up with the outrider around the pile of rocks. If he took that direction, he might reach the man too late to help him – already he could see the pointed shapes of shortbows held aloft by the pursuers. They were only waiting to come within shooting range.

Without thinking about it or pausing, he turned Saryu's head slightly, changing direction to aim for a point that would take him between the outrider and the pack of pursuers. That way he could head them off before they reached the outrider and hopefully before they were able to shoot the man down.

Yes, but it will also mean you will face them alone. A score of armed horsemen against a solitary Sudas.

He grinned. He had faced worst odds. And survived.

Yes, but you were just a Trtsu kshatriya then, unmarried, and uncrowned. Your only dharma was to fight and kill as many of the enemy as possible. Which you did, but at great cost to yourself – it's a wonder you even survived.

Three quarters of a mile out, and the outrider was slowing down for some reason.

Sudas cursed the man.

'Ride, you fool!' he muttered under his breath, spurring Saryu to go faster.

Poor beauty, she was already giving him all she had. To his surprise, she put on an additional spurt – perhaps because she had spied the other horses in the distance. She was nothing if not competitive, his Saryu.

He patted her neck with the palm of his hand, rubbing it in a circle, his sign to her that he was pleased. She snorted and raced the wind.

The outrider was definitely slowing. Sudas could not make out what ailed the man, but at this rate, the pursuers would catch up with him even before Sudas reached them. That was not acceptable! Already the ones with shortbows were knocking arrows and taking aim. Then disaster struck.

The outrider's horse slowed, bucked once, twice, a third time, neighed violently and fell over onto its side.

The rider toppled, rolling over and over in the long grass.

For a moment, both were hidden from Sudas's sight, buried in the long kusa stalks.

'In the name of Indra!' Sudas said through gritted teeth.

Arrows flew. He saw them shower down where the outrider and the horse had gone down. One barrage. Then another.

'You cowards! He's a lone man, down already! Face him with your swords if you dare, not shoot from afar.'

Sudas knew the pursuers could not possibly hear him over the sound of the wind, but something made them look in his direction, and he saw those in front turn in their saddles to speak to one another and all at once he understood: *The outrider knows something. They mean to kill the man before I can reach him and learn what it might be.*

Sudas snarled. 'Ride, Saryu!' he hissed in his mount's ear. She did not reply or respond – she was already galloping at full speed.

Less than half a mile now. Closing fast.

But already he could see that the outrider was doomed. The pursuers were barely a hundred yards from the spot where the man and horse had gone down, and neither had risen up again. That meant they were either injured, unconscious or dead.

Arrows flew again.

And again.

Sudas thought he heard the sound of a horse whinnying in distress, as it might if struck by arrows. But he could not be sure: The shirring of the wind in the ocean of grass drowned out all other sounds. The farther he rode out into the kusa fields, the louder the sound grew. As the wind increased in intensity, the shirring sound could become loud enough to prevent a man from hearing his own thoughts. Guru

Vashishta had brought him here often as a boy, to sit amid the high stalks and meditate. The omnipresent sound in the background, particularly this natural din, served to fill the back of the mind, blanketing all minor thoughts and little distractions that cropped up unbidden, clearing a space that allowed for perfect meditation. Sudas had fallen into his first meditative trance here and after that, he had ridden out often of his own accord. Every time he was troubled or harried by the daily problems and responsibilities of his position, he came to Uttunga and the kusa fields. One allowed him to meditate peacefully, the other enabled him to contemplate the infinite possibilities and hopes of the future.

But now, the song of the kusa grass was an obstruction. It prevented him from hearing vital sounds and voices that could give him a better understanding of what was transpiring ahead. As he rode deeper into the field, there were patches where the grass grew impossibly tall, high enough to conceal even a young bull elephant. It obscured everything else from view – there was only the sky above, grey and blue and cloudy in intermittent patches, and the blurring stalks of kusa all around, brushing against his face, his clothes and his sides. His garments were already soaked through with the accumulated harvest of rainwater that lay on the stalks, and now he began to feel as if he were riding through a veritable ocean. Water splashed on his face as individual drops from the tips of a hundred stalks were flung at him by the impact of his riding speed. He could see nothing except the grass. It enveloped and contained him and he began to feel the way he had the first time he had lost himself in here, as if he would drown and never find his way back. At least this time, he was not terrified of what might lie within the grass; everyone knew it was filled with snakes and numerous other predators that lurked and hid and hunted, using its perfect cover. Right now, however, he was more concerned about the human predators hot on the heels of his outrider.

Less than a hundred yards, he estimated, careful to keep his mouth shut and head down, pressing against Saryu's mane. He braced himself for the moment when he would come upon the pursuers.

14

If the sea of kusa grass drowned out Sudas's vision and sound, it also did the same for his enemies. He had the advantage of being a solitary man while they were a group, and as such, needed to call out to one another and generally cause far more noise than he. He realised this and slipped off Saryu when he judged he was close to the place where the outrider had fallen.

He patted the horse, heated from her run but nowhere near tired, and whispered to her to be quiet and wait for him. She nuzzled his armpit with her snout, then his backside as he crept away. He grinned and glanced back over his shoulder. He was pleased to see that the stalks around her were at least a yard higher than her head.

Stringing an arrow to his bow, he crept through the grass. The shirring of the wind through the grass was still loud enough to drown every other sound, and the wind still too fierce, but as he continued, he occasionally caught a part of a word or sound.

Thwack!

That was surely an arrow, fired from close quarters. This was a good sign. If they were still shooting arrows, that meant they had not yet killed the outrider. He guessed they had not found the man yet. An injured horse would be relatively easy to spot, but all a man had to do was lie close to the ground and be very still. They could pass within a foot of him without seeing him, not unless they were staring down directly at the spot where he lay. And staring down was dangerous in the sea of kusa: These stalks were sturdy enough to put out a man's eye if he was not careful. The rainwater on the tips alone was enough to temporarily blind a man. Sudas had to hold the bow in both his hands, keeping them raised above his head, which he kept lowered, in order to avoid being blinded.

Thwack!

Much closer now, no more than ten or fifteen yards, although it was difficult to tell in the whispering grass. He took aim in the direction of the sound, and waited.

Thwack!

This time he was certain. That way, roughly south by southwest.

He loosed the arrow and instantly began to move, not at a run for that would have been fool-hardy, but using a loping shambling gait that served to protect his eyes and face while making himself a difficult target to shoot.

The sound of a man crying out came to him, clear and unmistakable even above the kusa song. His arrow had struck home!

One down.

He could hear sporadic voices and sounds now. The neighing of horses, shying away from the grassy snake-infested fields, the shouts of men confused, angry and impatient.

He concentrated again, listening to the sounds that appeared closest to him, and loosed another arrow.

Again, he began moving the instant the arrow left his bow string.

He was half a dozen yards away and moving fast when he heard another man cry out, then a horse whinny in alarm, the particular sound a mount made when its rider fell off.

Two down.

He used the sun – barely visible through a dense curtain of half-formed clouds – and Mount Uttunga's looming shape, to fix his position, loosing arrows and moving on. He estimated that he was moving around the group of pursuers in a wide circle, shooting inwards. He knew that there was a risk he might accidentally hit the outrider with one of his arrows, but he could not help that. If he did not reduce the odds, they would both die in here, and their bodies might never be found. Without knowing precisely where to look, even an army of searchers would only thrash about aimlessly. If they found them, it would only be by sheer luck.

But right now, he was less concerned with seeking or finding than simply killing enemies. It was a task he was born and bred to do, and in a very short while, he felt certain his arrows had found at least a dozen targets. All of them might not be kills, but at such close range, the men would at least be disabled.

Arrows came back at him as well, but always to the spot he had already vacated. Even if they understood his tactic – shoot and run – they could not know in which direction he would run next. He was careful not to keep heading in the same direction, doubling back, cutting diagonals, and at least once moving so close that half a dozen horses thundered past him, their riders yelling furious abuses at their unseen nemesis. Had they looked down, they would have had him, but thanks to the grass, they rushed past without even noticing. He had a glimpse of one large white eye and flaring nostrils as the nearest horse stared wildly at him. He could have reached out and patted the animal as it went by.

Finally, he knew from the change in sound that they had understood his method and taken appropriate action. He heard no more sounds, of arrows or horses or men. That could mean only one thing – they had dismounted and were hunting him on foot.

The rise and fall of the wind in the sea of kusa seemed to grow louder in the absence of other sounds.

He could not be certain of their pattern or movement. For all he knew, they might stumble upon him by accident or worse find the outrider, and kill him. It was imperative he learned what the man had to say that was so important as to become a threat to his life.

He moved in the direction he had seen the man

and horse fall. The sun had moved a little since then, and there were no landmarks tall enough to stand out on the vast flat plain, which made it difficult. But some sixth sense inherited from generations of hunters told him to head in a north by northeasterly direction.

He almost stumbled over the man.

The outrider was lying on the ground, two arrows sticking out of his torso and an ugly gash on his temple. A section of his scalp had been ripped and hung down, oozing wetly. There was dirt in the open red wound beneath. Like all head wounds, it would not stop bleeding unless bound but Sudas resisted the urge to do so.

It was clear that the man was beyond aid now.

15

T HE FIRST warning he had that the enemy was on him was the distinctive sound of a sword blade cutting through kusa stalks. It was a very faint sound, barely audible, but he had been listening for it, or for the sound of an arrow slicing through the grass as it sped towards him. It made a whickering sound not dissimilar to the wind blowing across the sea of kusa, but with a deeper, metallic pitch. To Sudas's keen ears, it was as distinct as the difference between a koel's high pitched yodel and a chini gurung's warble.

He spun away from the sound like a dancer pirouetting, raising his own sword. He had been moving through the grass with the sword pointed downwards and backwards until now, to prevent it from making a similar sound. He brought it up now even as he spun away, turned again on the point of his heel, and then threw himself towards the direction of the sound. All this without having seen anyone yet.

The enemy was still raking his arm back, following through on the sword thrust he had made when he approached Sudas from behind. He had probably expected to catch Sudas unawares and was not prepared for his quarry to turn and attack him from his non-sword hand.

Sudas cut him hard but shallow, pulling back the blow to avoid hitting bone, even as he kept moving, spinning around so that his own back rolled against the other man's back, then around his sword hand, cutting him again, lower this time. The man screamed and fell, already dying. The spray of blood from his arteries lay across the grass stalks in peacock patterns.

The other enemy soldiers were close by.

Sudas changed to a forward-running crouched action, bent over almost double, sprinting much faster than any man would dare in the blinding kusa. By keeping his head down, he shielded his eyes but was unable to see more than a yard ahead. It did not matter – the grass shielded everything beyond a yard anyway! The advantage he got was tremendous.

He burst through the grass upon two enemy

kshatriyas who were facing away from him. Using both his sword and his shortblade, he stabbed one in the right side beneath the ribs and slashed the other's groin without slowing – *chunk, slash!* – then they were behind him and he was out of their sight. Their screams followed him.

He changed his angle, running in a semi-circle.

Another soldier loomed from the grass, alerted by the screams of his comrades and naturally expecting danger to come from that direction. Sudas came at him from his flank, using both blades at once to deal double blows, roll on the ground, then come up running again. He was bathed in the sweetish dew of the grass, and bits of stalk were in his mouth and nostrils. They began to cause an itch in his ears, but when he went to war he was able to ignore everything else and focus on the task of killing and surviving, which were of course really one and the same thing in battle.

Another soldier, facing him this time, somehow prepared for his approach, sword ready and coming down to bear.

Sudas leaped.

He flew above the soldier's sword thrust, hacking down with his own at the man's neck. Blood spurted, splashing him with the man's warm lifeblood, which felt searing hot after the cold dew of the grass.

Flying momentarily above the height of the stalks, he saw three more heads in a roughly triangular placement to his right.

He fell, rolling to the left, spun around, sprinted in a wide semi-circle again – and came at them from their left flank as they were running towards the place they had assumed he must be in.

Sudas took one easily, chopping out his foot, then stabbing him in the throat as he turned, shouting with pain.

The second and third turned and were quicker.

He stabbed the second in the throat with the point of his sword, dispatching him instantly, as the third came at him with an axe. Had the man been smarter, he would have flung the axe. But he had probably thought Sudas was moving too quickly to chance losing the weapon and so he came at him as axe-men always do, at a run, with the weapon held sideways and upwards, ready to chop down.

Sudas ducked the blow and chopped at his hand. Their combined speed caused his sword to almost hack through the man's upper arm. Blood and chunks of flesh spattered Sudas's face, blinding him. He slid, slipped and lost his footing, sliding several yards away into the grass. The sword stayed behind, imbedded in the bone.

That saved his life.

There were two more men waiting just ahead in the grass that he could not have seen.

They were the smartest of the lot, waiting for him to come to them from any side, rather than coming at him.

They had not expected him to arrive sliding on the ground, below the reach of their swords.

He crashed into them feet-first, knocking both over. One tumbled head over heels like the clay toy Indrani was fond of playing with, the one shaped like a woman dancer with her hand on her hip. Indraut loved setting it up and knocking it over with his leather ball. The man landed on his neck and broke it with a painfully loud crack. He would not be getting up again.

The other one fell on his side, rolled and was up at once.

Sudas found his feet and turned to see the man coming at him with a sword.

He remained where he was, stone still.

The man had expected him to move to avoid the blow and to cut him down as he did so.

But because Sudas didn't move a hair, the man was forced to slow, adjusting his sweep – and by then Sudas was already within stabbing reach. He punched his shortblade into the man's chest, once, twice, and then a third time.

The sword came around, seeking Sudas's body.

And missed, falling out of the man's grip as Sudas slammed the heel of his palm into the forearm.

Both man and sword fell to the ground, useless.

Sudas moved back a yard, in case the man had another weapon and strength enough to try it, and listened.

After several moments, he felt certain that there were no more men left alive.

He had seen a brown blur when he had leaped and followed it now; he found a score of horses clustered together, nervous and near panic. That confirmed his count of kills as best as was possible under the circumstances. Twenty horses, hence twenty men, and he had downed all in the past few minutes.

Sudas came back to the last man he had wounded but not killed, deliberately.

The man was crawling through the grass, probably seeking the horses, or simply to get away. The grass was stained crimson with his blood, but was springing upright again, undaunted. It took a lot more than a man's weight to keep a stalk of kusa down.

Sudas caught hold of him by the back of his garment and turned him over roughly. The man was thickly bearded and quite young – there were no greys in his growth, like there were in Sudas's own beard – but apart from that, it was almost impossible to tell which tribe he might be from.

'Who are you and why are you defying Trtsu law?'

The man stared up at him with a dull but defiant glare. Blood bubbled up at the corner of his lips. Sudas's blade had pierced the man's lungs; he could see bright pink blood frothing.

He shook the man, slamming his head back into the ground. 'Speak!'

The man laughed at him then muttered something that sounded like a curse. Sudas frowned and bent down closer, watchful for tricks. He knelt on the man's arms and from the way the fellow merely grunted rather than cried out, knew he had only moments left.

'What was that, dasya?' he asked with deliberate

insolence. The word was merely a name for one of the Bharata tribes but it was similar to the word 'das' which meant servant, slave or subjugate, and the pun was often used by Bharatas against their own as an insult.

The man's eyes flared, showing that Sudas's barb had struck home. He repeated the curse he had muttered before, and this time Sudas heard it below the ceaseless whirring of the kusa.

Then the man's mouth filled with blood, which was soon oozing out of his mouth, smearing his face and running down his neck to be soaked into the earth. He wheezed one final time, then lay still. Sudas was left with only the grass and the word the man had spoken before he died.

The word was 'Dasarajna'.

Ten Kings.

16

PREOCCUPIED THOUGH he was, it pleased him to see Indraut and Indrani waiting behind the thicket for him as instructed. They were goggle-eyed and skittish but had their bows ready, arrows notched and aimed at him as he came around the bend.

Indrani exclaimed at the sight of her father, lowered her bow and said in a chiding tone: 'Told you!'

Indraut put away his bow and arrows with a stony face. 'We heard a lot of horses, it could have been anybody.'

'But I told him that you would definitely collect their horses and bring them with you. After all, horses, kine, uksan are the only real wealth we can possess in this world,' Indrani said imperiously. Then, with an abrupt change of expression, she asked anxiously, 'Pitr are you injured?'

Sudas shook his head, realising how he must appear to their eyes, even though the dew that drenched his garments had washed away much of the blood, many spatters and stains still remained. 'It is not my blood. I have no injuries.'

Indraut stuck his lower lip out in a gesture of admiration. 'Sadhu! Two score men and you killed them all on your own!'

'One score, uksan-brain,' his sister said. 'It was one score, wasn't it, Pitr?'

He nodded. 'We must ride back home swiftly now. I may go too quickly for you, but you must try your best to keep up, do you understand?'

'We shall be right beside you, Pitr,' Indraut said confidently.

Sudas nodded, glancing up at the mountain behind them. 'Guruji stayed on Uttunga?'

'Yes,' Indrani said, frowning. 'He kept digging, then he was very excited about something he discovered. But he walked us to the base point and made sure we were on the horses. He even watched part of the fight with us from there before allowing us to ride down here to the thicket as you had instructed.' So his children had watched him fight and kill twenty men today. He was not sure he would have wanted them to witness that. Kshatriyas though they were, and may someday have to face equally cruel odds, he would rather have them retain their childish innocence a few years more before the business of war occupied their minds. But there was nothing to be done about it, and little point criticising them for something that was not their fault – they just happened to be there with him when it happened. And it was what he did.

'With me!' he called out, turning Saryu's head homewards.

She needed no further urging, recognising his tone and the direction at once. She started off at a pace that he knew the children would be hard pressed to follow, even though both rode full mounts, not the ponies some rich lords preferred their children to perambulate on.

The pack he had captured from the pursuers followed instinctively, one of them carrying the outrider's body slung over it, and another carrying a pursuer's body. He had never been able to find out what had caused the outrider's horse to fall, but it hardly mattered now. All that mattered was returning home and confirming what that cryptic phrase meant.

He had a fairly good idea already, especially after overhearing the argument between Guru Vashishta and Guru Vishwamitra, but he still needed it confirmed. And the only way to do that was to return home as swiftly as possible.

Before what I fear is about to happen begins, he thought, urging more speed out of Saryu. She snorted happily and increased her pace. She always rode fastest when heading home.

He sensed the air of threat even before he reached the city. At the farmsteads outside the main township everybody was out of doors, milling around, talking, arguing, and several brandishing weapons. Evidently, word had spread throughout the territory. That was not surprising, the Trtsus were a close-knit tribe after all. Only a generation or so earlier, the tribe had lived together, in one enormous kraal, or township or city, whichever term one preferred. It was the increasing need for division of labour in order to best exploit natural resources that had prompted more and more families to move to other regions, although never more than a day's ride away. Some still felt that the old ways were best, with the whole tribe living together in one wagon camp – a grama, literally – close enough to know everything that happened and to pull up stakes and move on at the first sign of danger.

Many saw him coming, recognised him and waved or shouted to him. He waved them on, indicating that they should come to the city, but never slowed his pace. If he stopped to talk to these outlying families, he would take hours to reach home. And whatever dark plot was brewing in Trtsu territory today, its epicentre was the heart of his own city, he knew this as certainly as he knew who was behind it.

People turned anxious faces to him as he rode past. Many looked defiant, angry, and even teary-eyed. Nobody seemed to be going about their daily chores, which was indication itself of how serious the situation was already. He wondered how many had heard rumours or known more than just a little of what was brewing and yet had said nothing. He wondered how many in his own sabha and samiti had known and kept it from him. It was not that he had not being suspecting that something was afoot, it was the timing, and the apparent coordinated planning, that he had never expected. *Not like this, not today, not now.* Had he not just killed a score of Bharata men for no apparent reason except that they were trying to kill him, he would not have believed that this was truly happening.

The mood in the city was grim. He sensed it the moment he passed through the gates. The sentries were apparently trying to break up an argument that seemed about to turn ugly. Everybody stopped and turned when he approached, but even the sight of their chief – nay, their *king* – did not soften their disposition. If anything, he felt their eyes glare accusingly at him as he rode past. He glanced back to make sure that Indrani and Indraut were close behind. They were smart enough to keep their heads down and avoid meeting the eyes of anyone they passed, knowing that at such times, even a look or gesture could be misinterpreted.

Sudas's heart ached for his children, for his wife, for all the innocents who should not have their lives uprooted by the imminent calamity which would, in the end, probably cause them most suffering. It was always that way with war and conflict. Yet it was no less unfair.

Finally, it had seemed, the Bharatas and their brethren tribes had put aside their rivalries and differences and begun to live together in harmony. The wedding celebrations of the past several days had made him feel that things had truly changed at last. Now, he wondered how much of that shared camaraderie, drinking and carousing, had been a sham covering the real politicking and conspiring that had been going on all the while behind closed doors.

The palace complex gates were being pushed shut as he approached. There was a crowd outside the complex and it seemed to have reached the point where it would soon become an unruly mob. People were brandishing weapons and shouting ugly threats. The sentries bowed and saluted as he passed through, shutting the gates behind him. He heard his name called out several times with dark promises and though he knew the mouths speaking those words did not truly mean those things, they still hurt.

Kingship be damned, he had only sought to do what was best for the people, without harming or hurting anyone. But it was only natural that in a time of crisis, the first blame would go to the man at the helm of affairs. And in this case, it was him. Their *king*.

17

T HE DOGS were barking. He heard them all the way across the compound. They were still locked in the north hall, and unlike him unaware of any real lurking danger, but from the way they were barking, they were probably locked in alone. They hated that.

A group of sarathis and syces milled about by the southernmost hall, staring in the direction of the great hall. Apart from them and a few others going about their chores with obvious confusion, the palace complex appeared deserted. Or abandoned.

He dismounted and wordlessly handed the reins to the nearest man. The man fumbled in obvious confusion and anxiety, but bowed and set about his task, clearly relieved to have something to do.

Sudas strode towards the great hall. Passing the north hall, the barking tapered off momentarily, and he knew that Sarama had caught his scent. He heard her yelp hopefully, calling to him. But there was no time to go comfort her. He strode on past, up the steps of the great hall.

The doors were shut but unbarred. He kicked them open and felt them strike bodies within. Someone grumbled gruffly, turning to stare at the rude entrant. It was one of the Anu, axe in hand. He glared at Sudas and made as if to bar his way, but when Sudas lowered his head and came at him without slowing, he stepped aside, saying something in an undertone to the men beside him. They laughed.

The great hall was packed to the rafters.

He pushed his way through men bearing arms, drinking, even eating – one man was tearing chunks from a leg of lamb that appeared barely cooked. There were people here from all the tribes as far as he could make out, which was not unusual in itself, for everyone had come to the wedding festivities. What was unusual was that they were all mingling with one another, not huddled in groups as usual. He saw representatives of all the Pancha Manava, the five peoples descended from Manu via the line of Yayati – the Purus, Yadus, Anu, Druhyus, and Turvashas. But all the other major tribes were also present – the Matsyas, Panis, Dasas, Bhalanas and Bhrigus, as well as lesser tribes such as the Shivas, Pakthas, Visanins, Alinas, Anavas, Sigrus, Ajas, and, quite surprisingly, *both* the Vaikarna tribes. He could not recall the last time he had seen both of them together in the same hall, merely talking and drinking instead of tearing at each other's throats.

There were also individual lords without permanent loyalty to any tribe; these were the ones who believed in the old way, when all the tribes had roved the world in grama-trains, calling whatever place they happened to halt their wagon's home. Of these last, Sudas recognised Bheda, Shimyu, Kavasa and a pair of foreigners with unusually shaped beards whose names he did not know but whom he had seen often in the company of Anu. All told, he judged there must be a hundred lords and ladies in the great hall, on this main level as well as leaning on the railings of the upper level. He could literally feel the timbers creak and groan under the weight of all those powerfully muscled men and their weapons. Even the women were bedecked in jewelled finery and luxuriant furs – and were armed as well, in keeping with Arya tradition.

Anu was seated on the king's chair.

Sudas had barely been noticed yet, in his own great hall, the seat of his government and kingship. So rowdy was the conversation, the intake of victuals and wines, so preoccupied were the assembled nobility, that he was able to stand virtually unnoticed and observe the mood like any casual bystander. It was revealing. There were so many factions present whom he believed to be hostile to one another, and who on past occasions had had to be ordered to be kept apart – even forcibly at sword point – in order to preserve decorum in the sabha or samiti convocations. Now, they were talking civilly to one another, scowling and keeping arm's length distance no doubt, with swords in their belts and axes on shoulder slings, but talking nonetheless. That was an accomplishment!

Others, whom he had not seen in either the higher or lower council for longer than he could recall, were present as well, and appeared quite sociable, eating and drinking and talking as freely as they might have at the wedding festivities over the past days – although he knew that most of them had not been present at the festivities. Which meant they had ridden in especially for this convocation. But all sabha and samiti meetings had to be called by Sudas himself, as king, and he had not called for either council to be convened today.

There was a great deal of talk going on, the sound level rising to the point where he could have clapped his hands and not heard himself. Someone – a bushy-bearded giant with a huge belly – realised his pot of drink was drained and threw it at the nearest wall in disgust. The glazed pot shattered against the timber log wall but Sudas heard no sound – the cacophony of human voices drowned it out. The cantankerous giant was Kavasa, a free lord notorious for his appetites for all things – wine, food, women and war in particular, though the order differed depending on his mood and the occasion.

Sudas had mastered the art of staying silent and gauging the mood of a sabha, samiti, or social gathering as a child. Blessed with a garrulous father whose loud voice and bombastic oration dominated every gathering or occasion, from a relatively early age Sudas had discovered that rather than resenting Pijavana being the centre of attention, he genuinely enjoyed staying in the shadow of the illustrious chief, listening, learning, watching, seeing things most people missed. A child at a gathering of adult kshatriyas was like a dog – nobody cared who he watched or what he heard. He had learned most of what he knew about kingship simply by staying by his father's side and observing. Later, he consulted Guru Vashishta on what such-and-such meant or asked him to explain the complicated, ever-shifting political balance between tribes, clans, families, lords, even among individuals in the same family.

Theoretically, the Bharatas were one nation, in the genealogical sense of the term, but in practice, they were a handful of scattered tribes that intermingled with numerous other tribes and nations. 'Bone dice flung at random by Manu's hand,' as Pijavana had put it once. His father had explained at one sabha session attended by young Sudas how it was simpler for powerful, violent men and women to rule their individual strongholds, or as Pijavana expressed it, 'cuff and cudgel those within reach,' rather than leave their seat of power to chase after the recalcitrant. In the old way of doing things, a chieftain commanded through a combination of love, awe, fear and respect – those who opposed his power simply left the grama. There was no need to fight your lord or chief when the whole world lay out there for the taking.

The only reason why most of these powerful,

wealthy kings and chiefs could gather in this hall today and tolerate one another was because each of them possessed resources enough to last them and their dependents several lifetimes. None cared about what lay ahead or about the future of the Bharata nation – or any other nation for that matter. For most, there was no such thing, merely Bharata kings who roved freely, living as they pleased.

Abruptly, Sudas heard the noise level die down. He felt a change of mood sweep across the gathering, then grew aware of those nearest to him turning their heads, and of others staring in his direction.

He looked up and it seemed every pair of eyes was staring at him.

The talk subsided and then died out altogether. Only the distant barking of his dogs remained in the background.

The crowd around him parted and he saw the man seated on the king's throne, Sudas's seat by law, smiling down at him.

'Welcome, Sudas, king of the Trtsus, we have been expecting you,' said King Anu.

18

THE CROWD parted to let him approach the throne, but the expressions on the faces of the men and women who were in his way told him more than any words could express. They were not the faces of men and women who were greeting a fellow liege or even an equal, but merely another kshatriya or fellow Arya. Some were openly contumelious. The two men standing with Kavasa, Bheda and Shimyu, even brushed him roughly with their shoulders as he passed between them, making no secret of their hostility. He knew better than to allow himself to be provoked by such risible behaviour, but he glanced at the faces of some of the kings he thought of as close friends until this morning, and was not surprised when they avoided his gaze.

So. I am being singled out and separated from the pack. The solitary animal being prepared for slaughter.

He reached the foot of the wooden dais on which rested the thrones intended for the king and queen of the Trtsus.

Anu was seated on Sudas's throne.

Anu's sister, Sudas's wife Sudevi, was seated on the adjoining throne.

Her face was a blank to Sudas, neither displaying the defiance of some in the hall, nor the open insolence of others, nor even the embarrassed avoidance of a few. She merely looked at her brother and appeared to listen intently to what he said.

It was as if she were saying to Sudas: *Heed my brother well. Listen to what he says.*

Sudas looked up at Anu.

'It seems you are in my seat,' he said to his brother-in-law.

He spoke the words without inflection, as casually as if he were describing the weather or the time of day. He sensed the hundred pairs of eyes on his back, boring into him, but did not let them affect or influence his behaviour.

Anu grinned.

'Sudas, good to see you. What kept you? Bathing with the horses again? Or was it the dogs this time?'

Anu looked up at the hall full of royalty. 'Early this morning – almost last night, it was – I found our friend Sudas in the north corral, wallowing in a horse trough. Perhaps it was recommended to him by his great guru? Part of the modern new Vashishta-yoga regime, hey, Sudas?'

This was greeted by a great burst of laughter.

Sudas neither smiled nor reacted in any other way to this obvious insult. The Bharata tribes had once shared a common guru, but over time, philosophical disagreements among the brahmin class had led to a deep rift, leading to the Trtsus being advised and spiritually guided by Guru Vashishta and the Anu by Guru Vishwamitra. The rest of the tribes had their own preceptors but since these two gurus were among the most senior, they tended to represent the opposing factions of the age-old rivalry, with the other brahmins falling in on one or the other side. Still, for Anu to crack a joke at Vashishta's expense was low and unbecoming of any Bharata. So low, in fact, that Sudas chose to ignore it altogether. He was certain that Anu would like nothing more than to provoke him into taking Vashishta's side, thereby giving Anu himself justification to defend Vishwamitra. Sudas had no intention of getting caught up in a philosophical debate. To each his own, he had always believed and it had never troubled him that others in the world chose not to adhere to the same set of beliefs as his own; he only asked that they respect his own beliefs and his right to adhere to them in the same spirit of acceptance.

'Why don't you make yourself comfortable on the seat reserved for you?' he said now, indicating the seat set to the right hand of the throne, at the head of a row of similar seats reserved for the other heads of the sabha. After all, as king of the Anu, Anu himself was a senior minister of the Trtsu sabha. A similar seat was permanently reserved for Sudas in the great hall of the Anu capital. Even if the seats were merely a formality and rarely occupied, they still symbolised the respect and decorum that fellow Bharatas accorded to one another.

Anu chuckled softly, glancing around at the people closest to him, his cronies and closest allies. Beside him, Sudevi continued to stare studiously at her brother, as if memorising every detail of his profile. She had not met Sudas's gaze even once until now.

'I like this seat better,' Anu said, turning back to

Sudas. He leaned back imperiously, resting his forearm on the hand-rest of Sudas's throne. 'Besides, had you been fulfilling your dharma, I would not have had to sit and take these decisions today.'

'Fulfilling my dharma?' Sudas repeated. 'How have I failed to fulfil my dharma, in your opinion, Anu?'

Anu shrugged wryly, raising his free hand and opening the palm to suggest the question itself was irrelevant. 'It is a king's dharma to protect his people and ensure their survival, is it not?'

'More than that,' Sudas replied calmly, 'every king must protect and ensure his people's survival. A good king, however, must also see that they progress and thrive. Merely doing the minimum required is not sufficient. One must always aspire to do more than what is expected.'

Anu dipped his chin twice, making a show of admiring the response. 'Well spoken! Very wisely spoken! You always did have a gift with words, Sudas.'

He was about to continue but Sudas spoke before he could continue.

'I'm afraid I cannot match your glibness, Anu,' Sudas said. 'Let us come to the nub of the matter. Why has every king, chieftain, and lord been assembled here today? I do not recall issuing a call for assembly, either to the sabha, samiti or any other council. And why are you occupying my seat? As I just pointed out, you have your own seat reserved, you may kindly move there and be comfortable. If you have any business to address here, I shall be glad to hear it – after you move aside and let me take my proper place.'

19

Anu remained seated on the Trtsu throne.

'You forget, Sudas,' he said, smiling. 'This is my seat.'

Sudas narrowed his eyes. What new ploy was this? Or was it a practical jest of some sort? 'What do you mean, Anu? This is the seat of the chief of the Trtsus. I am appointed king. Only I may sit here.'

Anu looked around the hall, addressing the gathering at large. 'Is it so? Is it truly so, my fellow Aryas and friends?'

A chorus of gruff voices answered insolently, 'Nay!'

Someone shouted drunkenly, ''Tis your throne and your house, Anu. Do as you will!'

A round of laughter greeted this last comment.

Anu looked at Sudas with a speculative expression, and then turned to Sudevi. 'What say you, sister dearest? Do I sit here by right?'

Sudevi was silent for a moment. Sudas frowned, wondering what game Anu was playing here by asking Sudevi such a question. *And what is she doing sitting here beside him in the first place?* He wondered. For the first time since entering the great hall, he felt a pinprick of anger in his mind.

'You do, Brother,' Sudevi said softly.

Anu spread his hands, smiling brightly. 'You see? My sister confirms it. I am on my rightful seat. This is my place, not yours, Sudas. You may seat yourself anywhere else you please! Go on, go on. Make yourself comfortable. Consider this as your own home.'

Chortles and chuckles greeted this obviously insulting offer.

Sudas felt his back stiffen. This was going too far. 'Maatr of my heirs,' he said, addressing himself to his wife. 'Do me the courtesy of explaining what you mean. I seem to be unable to understand your brother's manner of speaking, which leaves a great deal to be desired by way of protocol and courtesy. Kindly do me the service of explaining how the Trtsu throne is now the seat of an Anu king?'

Sudevi kept her eyes lowered as she spoke. She was so far from the demure wife that it was evident she was communicating to him even through this action. *She's saying that she does not agree with or condone what Anu is doing and making her do, but she feels compelled to do so out of loyalty to him.* Even so, he felt another prick of anger, not at Sudevi, for he understood the pressure she must be under, but at Anu, who would make his sister participate in the public humiliation of her own husband. For that was the only purpose of this whole exercise, he knew now, to humiliate him, Sudas, King of the Trtsus, and by extension, his entire tribe. This was Anu's way of paying him back for all the times the Trtsus had proved themselves superior in so many ways – from their expertise with horses and dogs, to their skill at metal-working, road-building, house-raising, drainage systems, and of course, in the arts of war, which was what really mattered to a man like Anu.

Sudevi spoke softly, the hall growing silent as everyone sought to listen to her words: 'Our society is traditionally based on a matriarchal structure, as you know, Sudas. Under Bharata law, succession, inheritance and ownership of land and all possessions are held by the matriarch of any line. In the absence of your mother, may Sri embrace her eternal soul,

I am the matriarch of your house. Your rule until now, and your authority over all Trtsu matters, is at my behest and on my behalf. You know this well, already, dear husband, for you are as learned in the law as you are wise in its implementation. What you must also know is that under certain circumstances, I may exercise my authority as matriarch of your house and relieve you of your duties, in order to govern on my own. I hereby exercise my right to do so under Bharata law, and stake my claim to the throne of Trtsu and control of all properties and territories governed by you, on my behalf, including the people and possessions contained in those properties and territories. As is my right, I have asked my brother to assist me in these matters and appoint him as regent in my stead. He speaks for me and all he says is law by writ of the authority I grant him. I pray you, grant him the same respect, honour and obedience you would expect any Bharata to grant a king of the Trtsu. From this day forth, Anu shall be king of the Trtsu in every sense of the term.'

She delivered this whole speech, which had the air of a rehearsed and prepared delivery, with a painstaking monotone that made it clear she neither felt pleased about nor wished to be saying these things, but had no choice in the matter.

The roar of approval that resounded off the walls and ceiling of the great hall was in complete contrast to her icy formality.

'SADHU! SADHU!' the gathering roared, expressing their approbation in no uncertain terms.

A gruff voice, thickened by drink and fighting shouted hoarsely, 'HAIL TO ANU, KING OF THE BHARATAS!'

Sudas resisted the urge to turn around and look. He was sure the person who had shouted this last part was none other than Bheda, another roving lord and close friend of Anu.

The man who was the centre of this lavish attention leaned forward, resting on his knees, and looked inquisitively at Sudas.

'So you see, my dear brother-in-law, this is indeed my seat and I am here by law, at my sister's behest and by her authority.'

He gestured dismissively. 'I urge you to find yourself a seat and rest your weary limbs. I am sure you will have much to brood about in the days to come. Think of this as a well-earned rest from your kingly duties. Drink some soma, enjoy the hospitality of my great hall, and dally with any comely lass you take a fancy to. After all, you Trtsus are too obsessed with things like work, duty, dharma, sacrifice... you need to expand your horizons and enjoy yourselves a little.'

20

Sudas resisted the urge, not for the first time since he had known Anu, to punch the man in his long aquiline nose, hard enough to smash it sideways upon that bearded cheek. Instead he said aloud: 'You are mistaken.'

Anu looked at him with an amused air. 'You are the one who is—'

'Shut your mouth, Anu,' Sudas said quietly, too quietly to be heard by any except those closest to the dais. 'I was addressing your sister.'

Sudevi looked up for the first time. She looked startled but also nervous. 'Me, Sudas?' she asked, and he was relieved to hear her speak normally at last.

'You are mistaken,' he went on without preamble. 'The law you quoted is only applicable when the matriarch is without a husband or husband's brother to govern and manage her property and possessions. I am still very much alive and quite able to govern as well as manage all Trtsu affairs. You cannot dispose of me.'

He was pleased to see her face brighten at once. 'Truly?'

He took the last few steps up the dais, approaching her throne. She stood up out of respect for him, not as her king or husband, but because it would be ridiculous for her to remain seated and look up at his considerable height. He took her hands in his own, rubbing her palms affectionately.

'Are you well?' he whispered.

She nodded silently. Then she said aloud: 'Explain.'

'The interpretation of the law you quoted was intended to be used in exactly the opposite manner.'

She frowned, glancing over his shoulder and said, 'What do you mean?' in such a loud voice and exaggerated tone of incredulity that he knew she was making sure everyone in the great hall heard them as well. He matched his tone to hers.

'You are in fact the matriarch of my house by default, since I have no surviving mother or grandmother or even aunt, nor any sisters to claim ownership and authority over Trtsu property. But you are first and foremost the matriarch of your own tribe.'

'My own tribe?' she asked.

'The Anu,' he announced loudly. 'You are after all the eldest living Anu woman, are you not?'

'Aye,' she said formally.

'In that case, if you desire, you can depose your brother from his throne and take over all Anu property henceforth, simply by announcing your intention to do so, and you may even appoint me to govern and manage all possessions and people in your stead if you wish. Because Anu himself is your younger brother and born of a different mother than your own, is he not?'

'Indeed!' she said, allowing her delight to show in that single word.

'And if you feel he is incompetent or incapable of ruling or governing as wisely as you would, you have every right to replace him, and ask me, your husband, to rule the Anu in your place.'

'I see,' she said, and her bright brown eyes sparkled with pleasure as she added, 'Is that what you advise me to do, husband dearest?'

'Enough!'

Anu had sprung to his feet. He took two steps forward and from the look of unadulterated rage on his thin face, it was evident he would have liked to grasp Sudevi by her long lustrous hair and throw her aside. But Sudas was there, also within grasping reach, and Sudas met him with a look of his own, one that had caused other men to drop their weapons and flee on occasion. Anu settled instead for expressing his anger through words.

'I do not agree with this interpretation of the law,' he said. 'It is false, and incorrect!'

'What is the correct interpretation of the law, according to you then?' Sudas asked calmly. He touched Sudevi's arm, motioning her to imperceptibly move to one side. Understanding his meaning, she moved aside slowly, casually.

Anu sputtered for a moment, then finally clenched his fist and shook it at Sudas. 'What my sister said earlier!' he barked. 'That was the correct interpretation.'

'Really?' Sudas asked, turning his back on Anu to look upon the sea of faces in the hall. Any number of them, filled with hatred, anger and loathing, leaped out at him, but there were also some that appeared sympathetic or at the very least, eager to be seen as neutral. This was not as simple a coup as Anu had expected it to be.

He suspected that Anu's entire plot had hinged on a quick takeover, bolstered by the belief that he was acting under the perfect protection of law. That mistaken belief had clearly been given to him by someone well versed with the law and its interpretations. Anu himself was not a man of intellect or learning. Sudas suspected that a certain long-bearded preceptor was likely to be the one who had told Anu that this clever tactic would be indisputable under Arya law. What he had failed to tell him was that the same law could be used by both parties, and that if it came to a challenge, then the party with the closer blood-link would win. In this case, it was indisputably Sudevi, who as the eldest surviving woman of the house of Anu, could certainly claim matriarchal rights. On the other hand, here in Sudas's home, as his wife by marriage, her claim would be tenuous at best. For one thing, all he had to do was annul his marriage to Sudevi and she would no longer be his wife, thereby losing all claims to matriarchal status in his home and hall. Not that he wished to do so, but it was a valid point in law. On the other hand, her claim over her Anu home and hall was by blood-birth and that could never be denied.

But he knew that a long debate on interpretation

of Arya succession law would not resolve the real issue at hand. So rather than argue further against Anu, he simply said, 'In that case, let us put it to the sabha eldermen and ask for their vote.'

Anu was silent for a moment.

Sudas knew he really had no response to that suggestion.

If they put it to the sabha eldermen, the decision would take days, and the vote would almost certainly come in Sudas's favour. Anu's entire ploy was predicated on staging a dramatic overnight coup, yet giving his actions the semblance of law and respectability. And Sudas knew that Anu himself was not a man who cared a whit about law and respectability. All this had been only at Guru Vishwamitra's behest. By cutting down the legal footing Anu had sought to stand on, he had forced the man's hand. Now, Anu's true nature would have to reveal itself.

And it did.

Anu's eyes turned cold, his lips pursing tightly. All pretenses at bonhomie and benevolent charm fell by the wayside with the suddenness of a dropped hammer.

He drew his sword and pointed it at Sudas's throat. 'I think we have bandied enough legalese for one day. Let us settle this the old, honest way instead. I lay claim over all Trtsu lands and possessions. Who dares stop me?'

21

Anu laughed in the silence that followed – a relative silence, for even though nobody spoke, Sudas could hear the familiar sounds of heavy metal ringing, clanging, and clattering, as weapons were unsheathed or held in a firmer grip. He had no doubt that at least a hundred sharp blades were out and ready to strike in the great hall now. At such close quarters, in this enclosed space, it would be a bloodbath. Anu was laughing because he knew it.

'I recall you holding a sword to my throat only this morning, Sudas,' he said, teeth bared as he tilted his head backwards to look down his long nose at his brother-in-law. 'Now the blade is in my hand, and it is your throat that is at risk. How does it feel?'

Sudas's response was quiet and calm, just loud

enough to be heard by the listening assemblage. 'Cowardly.'

Anu's smile vanished. His lips closed and eyes narrowed. 'Did you just call me a coward?'

'Yes, I did,' Sudas said. 'For only a coward and a traitor to his own kin brings armed warriors into the great hall to stake a claim. A true kshatriya would have the courage to wage war openly on the battlefield, and give his opponent a fighting chance.' Anu's eyes were filled with an emotion that could only be described as venomous. 'You could fight me now. The great hall is as good a place as any. Disputes have been settled thus before. Perhaps it is you who is the coward, Sudas.'

Interestingly, Sudas noticed, nobody spoke to either support or oppose Anu's words. It appeared that the dispute, if one could call it that, had reached a point where those gathered were waiting to see what fared next, willing to wait for the outcome before weighing in on either side. *That means they are still uncertain about supporting Anu,* Sudas thought.

He decided to take a bold, dangerous, and possibly fatal step.

He turned his back on Anu. And on Anu's sword point.

He raised his hands, facing the gathering in the great hall, addressing everyone at large, raising his voice slightly while keeping his emotions in check.

'Would a coward do this?' he asked. 'Would a coward dare to turn his back on his enemy and risk being run through with a sword from behind? Would a coward ask for a battle on neutral ground when he can fight in his own hall, amongst his own people, with a thousand warriors at hand against a mere hundred of his enemy?'

Several of the angry, hostile faces frowned. A few hawked and spat. Others shook their heads reluctantly, conceding his point.

Sudas saw a familiar white-bearded face looking at him with a speculative expression. He gestured in the man's direction.

'King Angirasa of the Bhrigu,' he said.

The man started. He had not been expecting to be called out. *He probably thought this would have been over at the matriarchal succession ploy itself. He didn't expect swords to be drawn in the hall, nor for things to go this far.*

'Yes?' Angirasa said tentatively.

'You are an elder to Anu and myself, you were

a friend of my father Pijavana, and you knew my grandfather Divodasa too. You have seen countless disagreements, disputes, and conflicts of all kinds, raised and settled in various ways. Have you ever seen Aryas bring arms into the great hall in order to forcibly stake a claim on a fellow Arya's kingdom?'

All heads turned to look at Angirasa. The king of the Bhrigus glanced around uncertainly. Sudas resisted the urge to smile. Whatever Angirasa might have expected to hear and see today, this was not it. He was in a quandary now. Sheer courtesy demanded that he answer Sudas's question. Yet if his answer displeased Anu, it would affect the alliance they had undoubtedly forged. And if he blatantly lied and kowtowed to Anu, that would be regarded as cowardly and un-Arya in its own right. Not for nothing was the term Arya applied only to those peoples whose moral and ethical sense was finely developed and who answered to the highest standards of conduct. Once propositioned, Angirasa could only respond with one answer.

'Nay,' he answered shortly, clearly not wishing to say a syllable more than was needed.

But Sudas persisted. 'Why not? After all, Anu here seems to feel that it is quite acceptable to take what he wants by force – although only after he failed to do so through legal means. So what would be so wrong about simply cutting me down from behind right now, and then taking over my possessions and properties by violent force?'

Angirasa shot a heated glare at Sudas, showing his anger at being put in such a position. 'It would be un-Arya, against kshatriya dharma,' he said briefly.

Un-Arya. Against dharma. That was far worse than merely saying 'cowardly'. It was the greatest insult that could be levelled against any Arya kshatriya, to be told he was not worthy of being called such. Angirasa had not actually called Anu un-Arya or an adharmic kshatriya, but if Anu now went ahead with his aggressive coup, that was how it would be perceived.

A furore arose. A hundred voices began clamouring at once, some shouting, others abusing, and a few arguing hotly.

Sudas made no attempt to quell the clamour. He stepped aside and looked back at Anu. His brother-in-law had lowered the sword, it appeared, but if eyes could pierce like daggers, then his grey pupils would have stabbed Sudas to death right then.

'Well, dear brother of my beloved wife,' Sudas

said quietly, his words intended only for Anu now as the furore raged around in the great hall. 'It appears you would be the coward after all. Is that how you wish to stake your claim? Through illegal, cowardly and un-Arya means?'

Anu stepped forward until he was within stabbing reach of Sudas. Sudas held his ground and his gaze, keeping his eyes on Anu's face, not his hands. He had survived the past hour through words and reason, he would chance this as well. Besides, if Anu had wished to cut him down regardless of honour or tradition, he would have done so already, while Sudas's head and back were at the mercy of Anu's sword.

'You are a master of words, Sudas,' Anu said in a voice that failed to conceal his seething hatred. 'But on the battlefield, you are no match for me.' He gestured with a jerk of his long neck. 'For us.'

Sudas nodded. 'Perhaps. And perhaps not. Does that mean the Anu are declaring war against the Trtsu?'

Anu smiled. 'Not just the Anu, Sudas. Everyone.'

Sudas's heart froze. 'Everyone?'

Anu jerked his head again. 'Everyone is with me. Against you. We shall crush you like a newborn whelp beneath an elephant's foot.'

He turned and began walking down the dais steps. 'We are leaving,' he announced to his supporters. Turning back to Sudas, he called out, loud enough to be heard by all, 'We meet next on the fields of battle, Sudas. Where you will have to fight with sharp metal and a clever tongue can be lopped off before it can spout legalese. I shall see you there in the place of blood and entrails.'

With that left the great hall.

22

THE SKY had brightened during the time Sudas had been in the great hall. He had to narrow his eyes as he emerged from the torch-lit hall into the gaudy golden light of noon. Outside, aides were fetching horses from the corrals and the visitors were mounting them. Many were still uttering curses and abuses, some raising clenched fists and shaking them as they rode away. Sudas did not care about verbal threats. He was relieved that he had been able to prevent a blood-bath from taking place in the hall. It was not his life or even the life of his loved ones he had wished to protect, but the honour of the Bharata people. What would future generations say if the strongest tribes of the Bharata nation had fought one another in the very place reserved for calm talk and rational debate? What value would their children to come have placed upon concepts like dharma, honour, reason, if they had settled their differences through a mere brawl this morning?

Yet another part of him prayed he had not made a fatal error. What he had said inside was true: If he had to fight Anu and his allies, then this was the place to have done it, and now was the time.

He glanced back and saw Indrani and Indraut standing by the hall's entrance. Around them were a score of his finest archers. There were more behind and to the other side of the hall, archers as well as swordsmen and javelin-throwers. He had sent his children to alert his personal guard and bid them be ready for his command. A single man had entered the hall after Sudas and kept a careful watch on him. All Sudas had to do was give a hand signal and his men would have burst in and cut down his self-declared enemies where they stood. Surrounded and taken unawares, even the fiercest swordsmen and axemen could not survive a barrage or three by two score of the best archers and javelin-throwers among all the Bharata tribes. After the archers and javelin-throwers had downed the most dangerous enemies, the swordsmen would have moved in to finish the job. Within minutes, the great hall would have been filled with the corpses and mangled flesh of Sudas's opponents. The coup would have been silenced forever right there and then, leaving him free to declare himself king of the Bharata nation, or even samrat of the known world, if he so pleased. There would have been no military leader strong enough left to oppose him. The people would have followed him just as easily as they would have followed Anu had he succeeded in his convoluted attempt at a legally sanctioned overthrow.

I could have ended this here and now, he thought, tightening his fist around the pommel of his sword, which he had just finished buckling on.

But he knew he had done the right thing. That was the difference between himself and Anu – he was not merely a man of clever words, but he did believe that one must use sense, reason and verbal debate to try to resolve one's disputes. It was only the brainless dolt or the weak-minded craven who resorted to violence first.

And how smart am I now that I have to fight anyway? At least back inside there I had the advantage – even though they did not know it – and would almost certainly have prevailed. Now, Indra alone knows what odds I may have to face.

That was the first thing he had to ascertain: How many were going to war against him, and with what strength?

He saw Anu mount his horse, turning the stallion around so he could look back at Sudas. He looked over Sudas's shoulder and must have seen Indraut coming around the side of the great hall with the archers. He was a smart enough tactician to understand at once what that meant.

He urged his horse forward, towards Sudas, breaking into a trot as if intending to run his brother-in-law down where he stood.

Sudas heard Indrani exclaim by his side. He put out a hand to indicate to her that she should restrain herself. She obeyed at once but he still felt her anxiety. *I wish she did not have to fear that her maternal uncle might kill her father at any moment. She should not have to experience such a feeling.*

But Anu would not just ride Sudas down, that was not his way. Despite what Sudas had said to him, he was no coward. In court, Anu could be a boor, in polite society, even a brute, but at war he was a maha-yoddha, a champion among champions.

'You are a fool, Sudas,' he said, holding his horse

steady as he looked down. 'You place too much store on outdated precepts such as dharma and honour. I have always said they will get you killed someday and it seems today is that day.'

Sudas did not intend to reply but before Anu could turn and ride away, Sudevi came up and caught hold of her brother's stirrup, staying his horse. 'Anu! I beseech you. Don't do this. Sudas is your kin. Our children are your bloodline. Resolve things through the sabha and samiti.'

Anu smiled down at his sister through gritted teeth. 'This *was* the sabha and samiti. Because you are my kin, I tried to speak reasonably to your husband. But his sharp tongue and quick wit spurned my efforts at peace. Now I have no choice but to go to war against the Trtsu.'

'But why?' she asked. 'I have never claimed my share of our father's estates. Everything you have is yours alone to enjoy. You already possess great wealth, great power. Why are you doing this?'

He shrugged. 'Why do all men go to war? To amass more wealth, more power. The Trtsu seek to bring in modern ways, build great cities of brick and stone, turn the Bharatas into an earth-bound people.

We were meant to rove the earth freely, plunder and pillage as we please, take what we desire. We answer to nobody, no law, no *dharma*! We of the Anu have forged alliances with friendly Mleccha,' he paused, then corrected himself, 'with friendly foreigners and outlanders who will pay richly in exchange for free trade across Aryavarta. The Trtsu refuse to accept these profitable treaties. They reject every new proposal we bring to them that would enrich us all.'

Sudas could not let that pass. 'Only because your so-called *friendly* foreigners and outlanders seek profit at any cost, even the cost of Bharata lives and honour. They trade in slaves and barter human beings like they are seals or metal to be traded as one pleases. They do not respect our rules of self-governance, our sabha, samiti and other political institutions designed to use dialogue and rational debate. Instead, they resort to violence to get what they want every time. They pollute the rivers that sustain them, plant no seeds, slaughter kine and even eat them as a delicacy, and regard women as inferior citizens and objects of pleasure. Your fair-skinned Mleccha are barbarian outsiders in the true sense of the word. They look at this vast continent as just a treasure trove to be plundered, its resources to be exploited and used for their gain, regardless of the cost to life, dignity or honour.'

Anu grinned. 'And what do you regard this place as, Sudas? Don't you profit from it too? Don't you seek personal gain and wealth? Don't you wish to exploit the land and its gifts to enrich yourself and your people?'

Sudas looked up at Anu, silhouetted against a bright azure sky. 'I see it as home. And respect it as such. Whatever I take, I share with all the people equally. This is not just a place to plunder and profit, Anu. It is our home. Bharat-varsha.'

Bharat-varsha. The phrase instigated great revulsion or great pride in people's hearts, depending on their worldview. To Sudas and the Trtsu, it was a proud and noble ideal. Land of the Bharatas, from sea to sea, and mountains to sea again. A cause worth fighting for, and dying for.

Anu nodded sharply. 'So be it. Die here then, today. At home!'

With that, the king of the Anu turned the head of his horse and rode away.

23

SUDAS RAISED a hand to quell the debates raging across the great hall. At once, if reluctantly, all voices subsided. Those gathered here now were a very different group from the one that had occupied this same hall only hours earlier. The contrast was shocking. This group filled barely a fifth of the hall, and that included his personal guard and retinue. Even his wife's and children's serving girls stood at the back, watching anxiously. The mood was grim and tense.

All those I believed my friends, my allies, my neighbours, even those I have aided in times of greatest need, everyone has turned against me today. Why?

'I see that you are all that remain,' he said.

'They have all betrayed us!' cried Ambarish, his closest friend and most loyal confidante. 'They are all traitors and deserve to be executed. Pronounce judgment on them, Sudas, it is your right by law!'

Sudas smiled sadly. 'And what purpose will that serve, my friend? As always, your heart speaks louder than your mind. Yes, they have betrayed us. Yes, they are traitors to their own nation. But what good will it serve me to condemn them? They are still Bharatas, some of them. They are still our kith, even our kin.'

He gestured to Ucchasrava. 'You, Ucchas, your wife is a Gandhari in the Puru line, is she not? And you, Atharva, you are a gwala from the Yadavas who came to live among us and are now a kshatriya. Daha, your fair skin and light-coloured eyes proclaim you as a former Dasyu who came to love and respect our ways and now considers himself one of us. Salva, your sisters are all married into the Parsu and live in Parsa in the shadow of the Behistani hills. Bolan, you are of a Bhalana tribe who fought us, you alone survived as a newborn and were raised by our daiimaas as one of our own, and now you ride with us as a full-grown Trtsu. Thsang, Ravi, Veda, Kavi, Kuruk, Atharva, Parni, Assyr, Drahkyu, Alena... every one of us is also related to or connected by blood, marriage or some other way to one or more of the other tribes. Even the terms Arya and Mleccha are but generalised descriptors that may be interchanged freely, depending on which region one resides in. To a Parsu, we Trtsus are Mleccha, while to the Alinas, even Purus are Mleccha. So long as there have been two brothers in this world, they have fought over something or the other, be it something small, such as a piece of fruit or a larger reward such as the best horse, or the comeliest woman. Men fight. They do not always need a reason. At the end, when my wife, his sister, appealed to him one final time, do you know what Anu said? He said that he goes to war against us to take what we possess, because he desires what we have. That is reason enough for him.'

'It is the reason why men like Anu must be destroyed,' Thsang said, his eyes deathly in the flickering torchlight. 'Ambarish is right. We must destroy them all. To the last man, woman and child.'

'AYE!' shouted the others, joining in.

Sudas shook his head, walking across the wooden floor.

He had not seated himself upon the throne, nor taken the dais, for he was not speaking to these men and women as their king, merely as one of the Trtsus. The dais was empty, the thrones bare. His children sat with their mother on the upper level, watching with faces that betrayed their anxiety. His dogs sat or stood around the hall, pleased to be free and close to their master again after spending the morning cooped up in the north hall. Sarama was by his side, tongue lolling from her mouth, gazing up at him as she watched him. Her eyes glimmered with that peculiar reflecting sheen that animal eyes have in the light; it was the same thing that made it possible for them to see in the dark. It made her seem wet-eyed and adoring.

'We seek to slaughter them to the last child,' he said sadly. 'Does that include your wife and her family, Ucchasrava? What about you, Atharva? Would you have us wipe out the entire Yadava race? Daha? You have been singled out and called names for being coloured differently from us dark-skinned Aryas – "Pandu" is one I have heard often from the mouths of children who tease you in passing – would you have us go forth and slaughter all the fair-skinned Mleccha in the world? Salva, shall we go to Parsa and kill all the Parsu we find, extinguish even their sacred flame in their temples of Agni? Once we begin, where shall we end? What purpose will it serve? What if we set out to slay all our enemies, and the friends of our enemies, and the kith and kin of those friends of our enemies? Then some day, in some distant age, we may find that we have been killing our own daughters and sons and sisters and brothers and wives,' he paused and glanced up at his own wife, Sudevi, 'only because of the blood that runs in their veins, the colour of their eyes or skin, the varna into which they were born, the river beside which their ancestors lived, or the colour of their krtadhvaj. When genocide begins, it ends at your own doorstep. For the wages of violence is more violence. The price of slaughter is your own death. There is no end to killing. Each new act of violence begets new enemies. Every drop of blood you shed strengthens their resolve against you. The more we kill, the more will rise up against us. It will only end with our own end.'

'So be it,' Sudevi said, startling him. 'If our own loved ones are the cause of our suffering and pain, then let us put them to the sword. Let us go on a rampage of slaughter, Sudas. Let us fight until they are all gone, or we are all gone.'

Sudas shook his head slowly. 'Nay, my love. You speak bravely and out of anger, for you feel betrayed by your own blood-kin. Am I not betrayed? We all are. Yet what good is such satisfaction that destroys our future? If you kill your brother today, what will you tell our children tomorrow? Shall we tell our future generations that we warred against one another and slaughtered each other, and therefore they must continue the slaughter as well, to avenge us? It will continue to the end of days.'

There was silence as everyone present considered what he had said.

Drahkyu spoke in his odd far-northern accent: 'What you say is true. A blood feud can only end in blood. But what else can we do now? Everyone has turned against us. Already we hear they are gathering for battle on our borders. Before this day is over they mean to invade our lands and slaughter us all. What other choice do we have but to declare a like feud against them? It is the only honourable thing left to do, is it not, Sudas?'

Sudas raised a hand to emphasise his own words, 'We fight because they betray us. We fight to protect what we have and what we believe in. They are the aggressors, not us. We shall defend our borders and our territories, we shall respond to their violence with like force. But we shall not launch a campaign of vengeance. We shall not let the cycle of blood and revenge go on beyond this battle. Whatever happens today, live or die, triumph or loss, we shall end it here and now. We shall leave our anger on the field of battle and come home to our pallets to sleep with clear consciences. Or we shall lie down on the field itself and sleep in pallets of bone and blood. But remember this, each and every one of you, we fight because we must, not because we want to. We fight to defend a dream, an ideal, an ambition. A dream of a united Bharata homeland. Bharat-varsha. That was the reason why we were building the city. That is the reason why they have turned against us. They seek to destroy the dream by destroying us. But they are wrong. For flesh can be sundered, blood can be spilled, and men slain. But dreams can be passed on from generation to generation. We fight today to keep our dream of a Bharat-varsha intact. And live or die, that dream will survive us all. They fight for nothing except their own lust for power, wealth and slaughter. That is what differentiates us from them. Do not forget this, any of you.'

He sighed and looked around, glad to see that some of the madness had dimmed in the eyes looking back at him, if not the anger and betrayal. 'Now, let us consider what little we have left to fight with, and what they are likely to bring against us.'

24

THE ANSWERS to those two questions were simple: Nothing. And everything.

Being so closely interrelated and intermarried, many who called themselves Trtsu had gone over to the other side. One could hardly blame them. The sheer scale of the opposition was so great, their numbers so formidable, it was not even a fight worth considering.

Sudas walked through the north corral, spending a few moments with each of his horses before preparing them for mounting. He did this personally because he loved them no less than he loved those who walked on two legs and felt they deserved his respect, his love and his attention. And he did this because this might be the last time they served him, for they were likely to be killed or maimed in the ensuing battle. For him, these beasts were no less than warriors in his cause, and no less deserving of his love and respect. He did the same with his dogs, for they too would be going into battle with him today. He needed every capable fighter he could find. Besides, if his horses and dogs were more loyal to him than most of his relatives and friends, then they deserved his time and affection.

The odds were chilling. After the arguments in the great hall, Anu and his men rode through the city, informing every Trtsu of the day's debate and its outcome. As a result a great exodus took place, taking with it a vast majority of the city's dwellers, who chose to side with the opposition.

The enemy was so confident of its superiority that before departing they had themselves left word of their strength with Sudas's people.

Three thousand three hundred and thirty-three score was the combined strength of the enemy.

In plain numbers, sixty-six thousand six hundred and sixty fighting heads.

The words whispered by the dying pursuer in the kusa grass that morning had been perfectly accurate.

Ten Kings.

Dasarajna.

The Anu, Pani, Alinas, Puru, Matsya, Bhrigu, Parsu, Dasya, Druhyu and Bhalana had all declared war against the Trtsu.

Their numbers roughly came to around three thousand score: sixty thousand men.

Siding with them was a motley bunch of individual champions, freeholders, rovers, marauders, Mlecchas, and self-declared lords and princes.

The Ten Kings desired to destroy the Trtsu, take their land and kine and possessions, and share them amongst themselves. The Anu, of course, would get the lion's share.

The rest simply wanted to kill and rape the Trtsus, in every sense of the word.

The goal was total annihilation.

The day chosen was today.

The place was the bank of the Parusni, just south of Trtsu territory – the place from whence the outrider had come fleeing, followed by a score of pursuers. He had probably been bringing word of a buildup of forces on the far bank, the reason why he was pursued and killed.

Had Sudas not spied the outrider, he and his children might have spent the morning on Mount

Uttunga unaware of the coup that was taking place in the great hall in town. Anu would have used his specious legal ploy to justify an aggressive takeover, Sudas's loyal supporters would have put up some resistance and been killed on the spot, and everything would have been over by the time Sudas and his children rode home.

But that was not what had happened.

And despite the odds, despite the sheer impossibility of the task ahead, Sudas refused to give in. For one thing, surrender would no longer be enough to appease Anu personally. He desired to see Sudas and his children grovel, beg and then scream in terror as they were each brutalised, tortured and finally killed. That was the sentence he had pronounced on them. As for his own sister, he had declared her as the prize to any man or men who fetched Sudas's head to him. She was to be made a whore for the victors, to be used and abused until dead.

Sudas finished grooming and feeding treats to the horses and turned his attention to his weapons instead. They were already well honed and ready for use. He was done in moments. When he finished, he sat back and thought of what lay ahead.

The forces loyal to him numbered barely three

hundred score: less than six thousand. Not even one-tenth of the enemy numbers. That included a few old veterans, women, and young'uns who had never fought a battle or even a serious blood fight before.

The only option left to them now was to fight and die honourably. Die they all must, for to survive the battle would be far worse than death. Anu would see to that. Sudas did not fear death or being maimed or grievously wounded. It was the lot of a kshatriya after all, and he had known and been prepared for it all his waking life. But to know that one's enemies were one's own kith and kin, brother tribesmen and clansmen, even fellow Trtsu…

He shook his head, not ashamed to find tears in his eyes. Tears were natural, they were human. It was the cruelty of men who sought to enslave, kill and slaughter other men or living creatures that was inhuman and unnatural.

He wiped the errant tears with the back of his hand. One rolled into the brush of his beard and he dabbed at the spot.

Sarama came up to him and licked at his beard, finding the salty droplet and licking it off.

He embraced her, kissing her on her furry head.

She whimpered softly and placed her paw possessively upon his thigh.

They stayed together like that for a long moment.

25

Sudas was mounting his horse when the rider came galloping into the palace complex. It was one of the boys who had enlisted to fight in the battle. He was out of breath and red-faced.

'King Sudas,' he said, falling to his knee in the mud. Sudas gestured to him to rise.

'It is Guru Vashishta,' said the boy. 'I was scouting the south kusa fields as instructed, laying low and seeking to spy at the enemy's movements on the far side of the river, as ordered. Unable to see in the grass, I went up the side of Mount Uttunga to gain a better view.' He added hastily, 'I was careful to use tree and bush cover to avoid being seen from the far bank as I went.'

'I understand,' Sudas said. 'Go on. What about Guru Vashishta?'

'He appeared out of nowhere,' the boy said excitedly. 'One moment he was not there, the next moment he was in front of me, raising his staff, gesturing to me to dismount and come to him. I did as he asked.'

Sudas nodded, signalling to the boy to go on.

'He bade me ride back to town and come straight to you. He asked you to put as many men as you could spare to a very important task right away. He said to impress upon you that time is of the essence. The given task must be carried out at once, and completed within the next few hours, before sundown. He said to tell you that he commands this by virtue of being your guru as well as preceptor to the Trtsu and to the Bharata nation as a whole, and by the loyalty he showed your father and his father before him.'

Sudas stared at the boy, wondering if he was hearing right. He glanced around at the circle of men also listening intently to the boy's excited report. They all looked as nonplussed as he felt.

'Does Guru Vashishta know that we are riding out to battle? Is he aware of the events of the morning?'

The boy nodded vigorously. 'Aye, sire. I tried to tell him everything. He cut me off after the first sentence, saying he already knew and that was precisely why his message was so urgent. He said this task he entrusts to you is imperative and critical. It must be carried out at once and you must delegate as many men as possible to ensure it is done effectively. He said to emphasise that time is of the essence.'

'Yes,' Sudas said, rubbing his forehead in bewilderment. 'I understand that part. But what exactly is this task?'

The boy told him.

Sudas listened with disbelief, then dismay. 'And he wishes me to take good fighting men out of my contingent to do... *that*? *Now*? Are you sure he realises we are about to fight a battle? A battle to the finish?'

The boy nodded again, sombrely. 'He knows everything, my lord. He said that unless you do as he asks, you will never win this battle.'

Sudas looked around, wondering if the whole world had gone mad today, and if so, what alignment of the gods and heavenly bodies had led to this day. 'Winning the battle is not the point,' Sudas began to say.

'*That is precisely the point,*' the boy said.

Everyone turned to stare at him.

The boy looked embarrassed. He was a clean-faced youth, barely nine, younger even than Indraut. Sudas wasn't sure he knew his name, it was either Raghu or Bhargu, probably the latter.

'Bhargu,' Sudas said cautiously, 'what did you mean by that outburst?'

The boy hung his head shamefacedly. 'Begging your pardon, sire. He bade me say that to you. He said you would argue that winning the battle is not the point, but that I was to yell back the response, "*That is precisely the point!*" I meant no disrespect, Rajan.'

Sudas waved his hand dismissively. 'Never mind that. What else did Guru Vashishta say?'

'That was all, sire. But he said that if you did not set about the task at once, then to remind you once again that time is of the—'

'—Essence, yes, I understand.' Sudas sighed and looked around. Everyone was within hearing range, more or less. They were as intrigued as he by the guru's strange instructions. But what was he to do? It made no sense at all. Yet he knew Guru Vashishta well enough to know that his vision was far greater and wiser than anything Sudas's own mind could comprehend. And the manner in which the boy had delivered that last part of the message had stirred something deep within Sudas. Those words were so familiar.

It is what Pijavana used to say, he realised with a start. When Sudas's father's advisors said to him, as advisors will say, that the point was not whether one won or lost a battle or a war, he would reply in just that tone: *'That is precisely the point!'*

He knew that what he did next might make no difference to the outcome of the rest of the day. Might in fact be seen as foolish and eccentric in the extreme. But he also knew that in any case, the odds were impossible. Five thousand or ten thousand or even fifteen thousand, it made no difference against sixty-six thousand six hundred and sixty. Besides, while he had no notion what Guru Vashishta intended to do with the materials he had asked for, Sudas also knew that the guru would not be asking for them merely on a whim. There was a plan afoot. A far-fetched, possibly impossible, probably improbable plan. But at least a plan. Sudas on the other hand, had nothing. What could he hope to do with odds of one against eleven? 'Do it,' he said to his men. 'Do as Guru Vashishta asks. Set about it at once.' He pointed at Ambarish. 'See to it personally. Take anyone and everyone you need. Make sure it is done within the hour and dispatched to Mount Uttunga.'

As he said the words, the world grew dark and he looked up to see that the cloudbank had finally eaten up the blue sky and conquered the sun. For as far as the eye could see, there was nothing but clouds now, dark, brooding and pregnant with rain.

In the distant south, thunder growled and boomed faintly, announcing the impending approach of a storm.

A fitting day for a battle, he thought. *At least we shall die under the watchful gaze of Indra himself.*

KAAND 2

1

Sᴋʏ ᴛʜᴇ colour of a grey cow carcass three days dead.

Clouds brooding over the theatre of war like gods awaiting burnt offerings.

Not a wisp of kusa or a neem leaf stirring in the gloaming light of the late afternoon.

A ragged line of Trtsus arrayed to either side of Sudas. White-robed, for it was the Trtsu custom to go to war clad in funeral pallor: *shvityanca*.

Each Trtsu on a horse facing the river, placed several yards apart from one another to present the illusion of a larger front.

Faces washed clean, foreheads daubed with ash, hair neatly combed and straightened with bone-combs, then gathered and tied up in knots on the right sides of their heads: *dakshinataskaparda*.

Krtadhvaj dangling limply on poles. Had Vayu,

Lord of Wind, chosen to remain absent from this fray? Or perhaps he was going to abandon them too? Everyone else had, why not the devas?

On the far bank of the Parusni a huddle of enemy soldiers stood around. A few spearmen, mostly bowmen, no horses. They were waiting. As were Sudas and his army.

Army.

Could a force of less than six thousand be termed an army? Surely not? It was laughable.

Even all six thousand, including women and children, would hardly be more impressive. He had known this, as he had known that the enemy would take time to cross the river and those crossings would need to be accomplished in batches, giving the rest of his force time to finish their given task and join him here. He thought of them as fresh reinforcements, even though their given chore involved carrying heavy loads all the way from the base point to the summit of Uttunga. After all that carrying and climbing, they would be tired. Hardly fresh. But they still counted, every last one.

As did Guru Vashishta himself. Not for nothing was he preceptor of the Trtsus – of the Bharatas – by right.

Vishwamitra might stake claim to being the preceptor of the Bharatas today, and his associate, Pasadyumna, son of Vayata may act as purohit for the Anu and Purus and other Bharata tribes. But it was Vashishta, along with his purohits Parashara and Satayatu, who were rightfully ordained to guide, mentor, advise and preside over all official rituals of the Bharata nation.

In a sense, Sudas mused, this battle was as much a battle between Vishwamitra and Vashishta for that exalted position. For, while the kshatriya varna ruled the known world, the brahmin varna thought of itself as being pre-eminent in all things that matter most. If one was the body and flesh of Aryakind – of civilised humankind – then the latter was the soul and mind.

He knew for certain that the futile but daring attempt to dethrone him at the great hall had not been Anu's idea. Anu could no sooner devise such a plan than he could understand the importance of strategy in a long and sustained campaign. It was one of his failings as well as his strengths. Just as Sudas may sometimes fail in limited tactics or lose a battle but remain unmatched in overall planning and foresight. Anu knew this and so did his allies and supporters. This was why he dared not chance a long

and protracted conflict. For given time, he knew that
Sudas would outwit, outmaneuver and outthink him.
It was only in a brief brutal battle such as this that
he could hope to win.

And with superior numbers.

Sixty-six thousand six hundred and sixty. A nice
series of sixes and one shunya lined up in a row. Against
a solitary six followed by three shunyas.

Those weren't just superior numbers. It was a
devastating majority.

One against eleven.

And at the outset of the battle, probably one against
twenty, so long as the majority of his warriors bent their
backs performing the given chores for Guru Vashishta.

One against twenty.

He turned as he spied movement out of the corner
of his eye. His lieutenants. All the remaining three of
the original fifteen.

Ambarish was heading the force that was
undertaking Guru Vashishta's task on the mountain;
he had taken Parni, Kuruk, Veda, Kavi, Ravi and Salva
with him, as well as close to three thousand of their
most able fighting men, for Vashishta's task required
the strongest backs and arms.

As if fighting a battle didn't! Sudas thought wearily but without malice.

Bolan, Assyr, Drahkyu, Alena and Atharva were off on individual or paired missions on Sudas's orders and were expected back shortly.

That left Ucchasrava, Daha and Thsang to stand with him in the vanguard, if it could be called that.

They were standing beside him, waiting for his attention.

Glancing at them, he realised how odd the light had turned. They looked as grey as the sky. The air itself seemed tinted with a strange lack of lustre, as if all life, colour and energy had been leached out of everything. The kusa grass that had waved so green only this morning – splashed with splotches of bright crimson – had faded to a dirty greyish green. The dark brown mud underfoot, the rich alluvial soil of the Five Rivers lands, appeared dull grey now, as though it had been carpeted with ash. Looking north, west and east, at the panorama of grey sky and faded earth, it seemed as if some epic pestilence had ravaged the earth, leaving a funereal cast. Even the faces of his champions appeared dull and corpselike. A flock of kraunchya birds from the pond nearby rose up and flew westwards, calling out, and some trick of the wayward light made them appear to be flying upside down, their cries muted and sickly.

He knew Guru Vashishta – or any brahmin, for that matter – would be able to interpret these signs as omens or portents of some impending disaster. For his part, he needed no interpreter. It was a dark and stormy day and they were at war with their own blood-kin, brothers and sisters. It was a day of doom, and he needed no omens to confirm that knowledge.

'Rajan,' Ucchasrava said.

Sudas waited for him to continue.

Ucchas gestured over his shoulder. There was nothing there except their long, ragged line. 'Perhaps we should adopt different tactics.'

There was no need for him to explain himself further. The point was obvious: With such a small vanguard, there was little sense in making a front. Even if the enemy crossed in small batches, once they massed on the bank and charged, the Trtsu line would break in moments. It was not a question of how bravely or fiercely they fought but of the disparity of numbers. A single horseman could not hold a length of one score yards against one score enemy horsemen. They would just ride through the Trtsu line and the battle would be as good as over before it had even begun.

'I am aware of the problem,' Sudas said. 'But we must initiate. Once we know the enemy's strategy, we shall change tactics.'

Ucchas did not reply. He looked towards the river. There was still no sign of movement from the far side. Thsang and Daha looked up at the sky.

'The storm god hangs over our heads, waiting to attack when we expect him least,' said Thsang, speaking in the lilting tones of his people from the north, the land of the highest peaks in the Himavat range.

Daha made a strange sound in his throat. It was a curse word in his mother tongue – he came from the barbaric but brave horse tribes that roved the steppes, the vast unforested grasslands beyond the Himavat.

'The storm gods take no sides in the wars of men,' he said in his harsh dialect. Sudas understood only a phrase in the sentence, but deduced the rest from the context.

Sudas added reassuringly, 'Our patron deity is Indra, Lord of Storms. If he is going to take any side today, it shall be ours.'

2

THERE WAS still no movement across the river when the others began to drift back, one by one, arriving in short succession.

Atharva was the first to return, bearing exactly the news Sudas had expected – no movement on the northeast border. That was hardly unusual. The rivers hemming in that side of Trtsu territory merged in a raging confluence that was unfordable at this time of year. Nobody, not even the most lustful Mleccha raiding party, would be suicidal enough to throw themselves at the mercy of that monstrous spate. Boats, horses, rafts, even overhead tree-to-tree rope bridges, nothing could withstand the power of that torrent. Still, there was a slim chance that the enemy might have slipped men across weeks earlier in preparation for this day and kept them hidden until the crucial battle, for a flank attack. Unlikely, perhaps, but not impossible. This tactic had been employed twice before; once to annex a neighbouring region, and another time as a means of slow invasion. In both cases, the Anu had secretly infiltrated the other party's borders beforehand and lain hidden until the crucial moment.

It was better to know for certain than to be surprised in the heat of the battle. Without accurate intelligence, no strategy could be effective. And strategy was all the Trtsu had now.

'They are raging today,' Atharva said, shivering slightly from his ride along the banks of the confluence. He was the youngest of Sudas's lieutenants and had been struck by a shivering fever three monsoons past. The fever and shivers still took him on particularly wet days. 'They are at war with one another. You could hear their voices, raging and ranting.'

Sudas realised he was referring to the river goddesses. Every river was a powerful devi at arms, for rivers provided sustenance, nourishment, life itself. Therefore they were feminine and godlike. They also took lives, often arbitrarily and violently, even sweeping away entire settlements and devastating crops and herds of kine. Therefore they were warrior goddesses. Sudas was familiar with the phenomenon that had unnerved Atharva – the northeastern boundary of the Trtsu lands, where the rivers merged, was a rocky escarpment. The individual goddesses each tumbled, one by one over the plateau, cascading from various heights, to dig deep hollows in the solid rock below, creating a vast basin-like area, much like a natural dam. This body of water was fraught with powerful undercurrents, for the rivers were still in spate and moving downwards. At one point, they all burst free of the basin and shot through a ravine that often filled to the top during the height of the monsoons.

Atharva had ridden along the edge of the Trtsu side of this ravine, and in the channel below, where the dammed water burst through and shot forward, resuming its long journey to the ocean, the enclosed rock walls and grinding boulders could often sound like gods gnashing their teeth – or, as Atharva had just suggested, goddesses raging war with one another.

Sudas caught hold of the young man's reins, leaned over and clapped his palm to Atharva's forehead. He felt as if he had laid his hand against the side of a pot filled with boiling water. Atharva's eyes were yellow and his skin had a faint yellow hue despite the deathly grey light that lay upon the world.

'The sickness is on you again,' he said. 'Go make your horse lay down and rest in his warmth.' It was an effective way to keep warm out of doors.

But the young lieutenant only glared at his king and snapped the reins out of Sudas's hand. 'We shall all lay down together or not at all,' Atharva said shortly.

Sudas realised that he had already offended the young warrior. To say more would be to imply that Atharva was unfit to fight in the battle. For a Trtsu, the only thing worse than death was dishonour. To lie down and rest when one could be fighting alongside one's fellows was to ignore one's dharma. And to ignore dharma was the worst dishonour of all.

Sudas said no more. Had the young man been wounded at battle, he would not have told him to rest. This was a fight to the finish and every last one of them knew it. Sick or well, fighting was fighting and dying was dying.

Drahkyu, Bolan and Alena had ridden up while he was listening to Atharva's report and speaking with him. Assyr returned while he was debriefing the others.

Bolan motioned to the others to go ahead, electing to hang back to be heard last.

Drahkyu was morose as he reported that all the settlements on the northwest border had been raided and burned. The settlers who lived there were all hardy survivors of previous battles who chose to reside in solitary kinship with other survivors of their kind rather than in the crowded bustle of the main township. Over time, many formed loose friendships, even banding together in a kind of extended family, and the unwritten rule among them was to always go to one another's aid, whatever the crisis or odds. Drahkyu had seen a large number of charred human remains in the burned ruins of the larger kine shelters that were shared communally by the settlers to keep their kine warm and safe during inclement weather. The embers had still been smouldering, even burning slowly in some spots, and since it had rained heavily the previous day, that could only mean that the fire had been set ablaze this very day.

'The enemy must have raided them on the way out,' he said sadly, 'for I found large numbers of mount tracks leading from the town to the settlements and then onwards. They killed whomever they could, forced the rest into the shelters and burned them down on their heads.'

Sudas nodded grimly. It was a tactic employed by the Purus, who preferred the use of fire as a weapon and the cruelty of cremating their enemies alive. There were even reports that some Puru kings had set their rivals ablaze in their homes even as they slept, the easier to do away with problems of succession. He was sorely disappointed for he had depended on the aid of the settlers if the strategy he had in mind for the coming battle was to work. 'Did you follow the tracks that let onwards?'

Drahkyu wiped his face. It was stained with ash from sifting around in the remains in search of his friends – he had been close to many of the settlers, Sudas knew – but in the gloaming light it seemed only to soften his hard angular features. 'Aye. They led to the river.'

Sudas frowned. 'The river?'

Drahkyu shrugged. 'They must have used boats to get across and away.'

Sudas was still frowning when Alena began speaking. If the enemy had finished slaughtering the settlers that morning or even that afternoon, after they had led the mass exodus out of the city, they could simply have ridden out this way and crossed the

Parusni at this point where it was lowest and most easily traversable. Why cross the Vipasha up there where it twisted and turned in on itself numerous times? Yes, boats could have taken them across, but the crossing would have been treacherous at that point. What's more they risked losing their horses that panicked at crossing such fierce waters and were often crippled or killed in the process. It did not make sense. Then again, not much that was happening today made sense.

Alena was saying, 'The western border is clear but across the rivers I could see enemy movements. They were travelling southeast.'

That made perfect sense. The enemy had been travelling here, to join battle with the Trtsu on this front, as had been agreed. That gave him a great sense of relief for it suggested that for once Anu and the Purus – as well as the Bhrigu, Ajas, Sigrus and Yadus – were being uncharacteristically honourable. Well, he thought sourly, they could afford to be, with their greater numbers.

'Their numbers were more or less as we were told?' he asked Alena.

Alena looked at him as he shook his head slowly. 'Not even close.'

The others crowded their horses in closer, peering at Alena's face to glean his meaning. Several began firing questions.

Sudas held up his hand. 'What is it you mean to say, Alena? The enemy numbers you saw across the river, were they more or less than what we were told?'

Alena released a deep breath and said, 'More, much more. If that number was accurate in any measure, it must be only their main yoddha force. The movements I saw were of at least a full akshohini.'

'Did you say a full akshohini?" Daha asked incredulously. 'Including *chariots*?'

'Footsoldiers, cavalry, chariots, and *elephants*,' Alena said. 'A full fighting regiment.'

A shocked silence followed his words.

Into this silence, Bolan added in his rasping hoarse voice, 'And that is not the worst.'

3

ATHARVA LAUGHED hysterically. 'A full akshohini, with elephants and chariots, and he says it's not the worst!'

Even mild-mannered Ucchas who was rarely provoked, looked sharply at Bolan and said, 'What could be worse, Bolan? We thought we were outnumbered perhaps ten to one, now we find it is closer to a hundred to one. Surely nothing could be worse than that!'

Bolan looked at Ucchas without offence. The Bhalana was a man who had seen – and done, Sudas knew – some of the most terrible things human beings could possibly do to one another. The horrors he had witnessed, experienced and, to some extent, perpetrated during those harrowing years of his youth had left him with an emotional carapace, as if each atrocity had scarred his very soul, and the emotional scar tissue had hardened over time, leaving him with this leathery outlook on the world. His bald head and pockmarked face jutted from his bull neck much like that of a turtle.

'The enemy has been planning this attack for many months, perhaps over a year,' he said.

Atharva, visibly feverish now, giggled. 'What gave you a clue?' He said, then hiccupped loudly.

Sudas held up a palm, chest high. Atharva subsided as did the others, although their eyes danced with emotions. The situation had already seemed hopeless, now it was several steps beyond madness.

'Go on, Bolan,' Sudas said calmly, knowing that he needed to keep his lieutenants in check. The rest of their meagre force could not help but hear much of what was being discussed here and word was being passed across the kusa fields. If they were not cautious, there would be panic. Brave as the Trtsus were, they were not fools. Fighting odds that would have made most tribes quail was one thing; fighting odds that were impossible even for the devas was another. There came a point when even the world's bravest soldiers knew they must turn tail and run away in order to survive and fight another day. Sudas himself knew that Alena's sightings meant that he would have to seriously consider the option of flight, no matter how humiliating it might be.

Bolan continued. 'I rode to the extreme north as instructed by our rajan. There I found evidence of timberworks.'

'Timberworks?' Drahkyu repeated.

'Yes. Not on our side of the rivers but on the far side. I could not cross to confirm it but there was enough visible evidence to remove all doubt. The number of trees cut and the extent to which the wood cover on the foothills was depleted suggested a long and well-planned exercise. There was enough timber chopped to build a city – several cities.'

The others looked at one another. Assyr arrived at around this point but stayed on the outskirts of the group, knowing better than to interrupt. He looked despondent and flushed from the ride, a muted grey in the still sickly light, but not excited or impatient. Sudas took that to mean that his report was not urgent and could wait a few moments longer. He was keen to have Bolan finish.

'I do not comprehend,' Daha said. 'What could this mean?' Ucchasrava scratched the side of his neck, beneath his beard. 'Siege works?'

Atharva giggled but caught himself almost at once. The others took the question seriously. Sudas noted that he would have to do something about Atharva, the young man's fevered brain might put him and his comrades in danger during the battle.

Aloud he said, 'With numbers that strong, where is the question of a siege?'

Bolan looked at him. 'I think Rajan knows what the timber signifies.' Everyone looked at him.

Sudas nodded. 'I have seen this before. In the time of my father's father, when I was but a boy.' He gestured in the direction of Trtsu land. 'The rivers did not always flow as they flow now. Their courses change and reverse and change again, depending on various factors. At times, we have changed their courses as well.'

'You speak of channelling, Rajan?' asked Daha quietly. 'Digging new routes to make the river flow a certain way, to avoid flooding one's fields or homes?'

'Yes. But more effective than channelling is damming. That is what I think the enemy has been up to in the north.'

'Damming?' Thsang asked. 'We have a great dam up in our mountains. In winter it freezes over partly, like a glacier and our children cross it on special sandals with blades underneath,' he uses his hand to demonstrate a sliding motion. 'When the tribes of the foothills trouble us overmuch, we simply release the dam waters and drown their homes. When they made peace with us at last, we agreed to release water for their fields and not to drown them, so long as they kept the peace.'

Sudas nodded. 'I think what the enemy has in mind here is more than providing water for our fields.'

He gestured at the river behind himself. 'That is the reason why they are not crossing yet. They do not intend to use the ferry rafts to come across.'

Alena frowned. 'Then…'

'They mean to dam the river when they are ready to attack, and simply ride across the riverbed to attack us,' Sudas said. He looked around. 'They mean to take away our main strategic advantage – the river borders. Without the rivers to keep them out, our numbers are too few to stop them coming into Trtsu land. They will simply roll across us like a Jagannath, crushing us beneath their wheels and hooves.'

'With elephants and chariots,' Drahkyu said. He cursed in his language. 'Mitra, help us! It is like a herd of bulls battling a handful of dogs. We have no chance of surviving.'

'We already expected that,' Ucchas said. 'We fight for the idea of a united Bharata nation, as Rajan said.'

'That is true,' Sudas admitted. 'We fight for an ideal that we wish every Bharata would believe in. The hope is that even by dying, we can make an example of our sacrifice, and inspire other Bharatas to rise up and fight for the unification of the tribes.'

Several heads were nodding slowly in agreement. His heart ached to see them. Here he was talking about the extinction of their lives, their families, their homes, everything they held dear in this world, and they were agreeing with him. *By Indra, why do you give me this burden to bear? If this is all it means to be a king, I wish I had never been born your son, Pitr!*

In response, the image of a hoary face with the white beard flecked with a few last spots of black opened his mouth, displaying broken teeth, and laughed silently.

In the distance, thunder growled. It was a slow deep rumble, far to the north.

He took a deep breath. It was time. He must tell his men that though their cause was righteous and their actions just, dying was no good when it did not serve the purpose. With such a great force pitted against them, it was more likely that the extinction of the Trtsus would serve as a cautionary tale rather than a shining example. Others who believed as strongly in the ideal of a united Bharata nation would point to this field and say, '*They died for nothing, why should we?*' By losing this battle, they would lose the very ideal they fought for. Only victory could change that, only winning the battle could inspire others to follow in their steps. Winning *was* precisely the point of this sacrifice, for even if they died fighting here, as long as they won, it would be a tale that would be told and retold.

And impossible as the odds had seemed before, he had still held some small ember of hope within his fist. Now, it was extinguished completely. This was no longer a battle against impossible odds. It was a slaughter. A sick calf caught in a canyon by wolves had a better chance of survival or victory. With such a great force against them, they would not only be crushed, their ideal would be crushed with them. Nobody else would dare speak of a Bharata nation again, for fear of being wiped out as the Trtsu were. All Anu would have to do was say the word 'Trtsu' and people would subside and be silenced.

Sudas began to speak, to explain these things to his men, to make them understand why the time had come to withdraw and retreat, to flee wherever and however best they could, to save themselves and those they cared about while there was still time.

But before he could say more than a word or two, a shout came from one of the Trtsus farther along the line.

4

'THE RIVER is dying,' someone cried out.

Others along the line were shouting and pointing as well.

So it begins.

Sudas spurred his horse, his lieutenants following, and broke free of the frontline.

Most of the Trtsus manning the vanguard also followed but he did not bother to order them to stay. He had never been a commander who prided himself on decorum and protocol, not when they were maintained merely for the sake of appearances. Divodasa, his father's father had been such a general and Sudas's father Pijavana and grandfather had butted heads more than once over such matters. In the end, Sudas had learned to walk a practical middle path: Maintain decorum and discipline when they mattered. Relax the rules when circumstances did not call for them.

Under these circumstances, the last thing that mattered was holding a line, maintaining the appearance of a vanguard, keeping banners aloft and all that. Right now, the only thing holding these beleaguered men was their sense of brotherhood, and if that bond was strengthened by a relaxing of rules, he was happy to break every rule.

He had positioned his line half a mile away from the Trtsu side. Now he covered that distance in a few moments. Even as he rode towards the Parusni he could see that the river had weakened considerably. He realised now that it had been weaker than usual that morning as well, but he had been too preoccupied to realise it. It should have been fiercer than it had been this morning, after the rains of the past several days. Instead, it had been perhaps three-fourths its usual strength. Now, it was barely a third, and diminishing fast even as he approached.

There were enemy troops on the far bank.

Lines upon lines of cavalry were arriving in succession and turning heads to face the river. They filled the line of sight for at least half a mile and were closely packed. At one horse every three yards, that made around three hundred in each line, and he could see the lines piling up thicker and faster than he could count. Easily two or three thousand already, and who knew how many more were lining up behind – it was impossible to tell from where he stood.

He glanced back at the peak of Mount Uttunga, sombre and grey in the wan light.

He then turned to look at his men as he rode, 'Daha, ride to Uttunga. Go as far up as you need to, to see across the river. Come back with a headcount of the enemy.'

Daha swung his horse around without a word and rode away, but Sudas saw Ucchas and Drahkyu exchange a glance.

He knew what they were thinking: What is the point of a headcount when the numbers against us are so great? A hundred thousand or five hundred thousand, it made no difference. An elephant needs but one foot to squash a rabbit. What does it serve the rabbit to know there are three more feet capable of achieving the same feat?

Sudas knew that his methods might be futile under the circumstances, but any king's methods would be futile too. He had to hold on to what he believed in.

His faith was all he had. And his entire existence, his survival was founded on the principle of knowledge: To know was to understand, to understand was to engage, and to engage was to live fully. Anything less was merely animal existence.

They reached the bank of the river and he held up his hand to call a halt.

The river was reduced to little more than a trickle. From bank to bank, at its full spate, even at this – its weakest point – it usually covered a span of no less than one score yards. Now, the rivulet at the bottom of the bed was barely five yards across, and slowing further. In a few moments, it would stop altogether, he estimated. And the enemy could cross freely at a dozen points if they so desired. He could see only cavalry ahead on the opposite bank, but now that he knew there were other regiments, he understood that they had been positioned upriver.

That was what he would have done had he possessed such resources – throw the cavalry at the Trtsu in successive waves, while the slower footsoldiers and elephants crossed upriver and outflanked them; then send the chariots around downriver – perhaps even around the base of Uttunga – and catch the last of the Trtsu in a double-clawed pincer from which there could be no escape.

Anu and his allies did not merely intend to take all that the Trtsus possessed, they intended to wipe the tribe out to the last man, woman and child. Which was not hard to do, since barely a handful of them were left in any case.

It could even be argued that this was not against the rules of kshatriya dharma, for Anu had indeed attempted dialogue and even issued a challenge. With such a small handful resisting, it was they who would be termed the rebellious fools.

Except for the fact that I am the legitimately appointed king and spokesman for the tribe and as such, the chief of the Bharatas as a whole.

And even if Sudas alone stood on this side of the river and defied the combined might of all the known world, he would still be in the right and they in the wrong. And they had known this and had also known that he would never yield.

That is why they bring this great force against me, not merely to wipe out my people, my cause and even my seed, but to teach a lesson for generations to come –

Might rules.

Right fails.

It was a lesson he was not prepared to learn just yet.

He watched as a group of riders came galloping from the northwest, slowed at the bank and then halted. This group was visibly different from the endless lines and rows of riders beyond them. They rode at a slower statelier pace, their horses were saddled with banner cloth corresponding to the various krtadhvaj on the poles behind them. They wore burnished bronze armour exquisitely made and carved with fine filigree work – the patterns were visible even at this distance – and had a general air of authority about them.

These were not kshatriyas or even yoddhas. These were generals, commanders, kings.

He counted almost half a score of them. Then corrected his first impression as they straightened their line and turned to face the river.

Not almost, *exactly* half a score. Damn this pasty light, as dusky as twilight even though there were still hours to go before sundown.

Anu was among them, Sudas saw. Dressed in his proud bronze armour which gleamed even in this ashen light.

With him were the same friends, neighbours and

allies that Sudas had raised cups with, eaten with, laughed and talked and danced and sang with these past days during the wedding festivities and for years earlier as well.

The ten kings, just like the man he had killed in the kusa grass that morning had said before he had died.

The kings of the Anu, Pani, Alinas, Puru, Matsya, Bhrigu, Parsu, Dasya, Druhyu and Bhalana.

Ten Kings.

Dasarajna.

5

Anu and his fellow kings urged their horses forward, moving slowly towards the edge of the bank.

Sudas did the same. His lieutenants followed him. The other Trtsus stayed back.

Both groups of commanders stopped at the edges of the opposing banks of the dwindling river.

A distance of one score yards separated them now.

The air was as still as before, not a breath of wind stirring. The river's roar was silenced, reduced to a chuckling trickle. Except for the occasional growl of thunder in the far north, too distant to matter, no other sounds were audible. Even the flora and fauna of the region seemed to be hushed with anticipation, waiting. More likely, they were in hiding or had fled before the appearance of such large numbers of men and mounted beasts. Either way, it was possible to speak loudly and be heard across the river now.

'Sudas!' Anu called out, then laughed.

He looked around at his companions, who joined him in an impromptu burst of laughter. They all seemed jovial, in high spirits – quite likely in both senses of the term, for in these circumstances it hardly mattered whether or not they were intoxicated or sober.

Any drunk general could lead that army against us and win today, Sudas thought morosely. He did not let himself be goaded by the laughter of his opponents and knew his men would not be goaded either.

Anu collected himself and continued.

'Sudas, we can end this even now,' he said, smiling openly. 'This is no battle, it is a travesty. Tell your men to drop their arms and ride away, go into exile as far from these lands as possible, and they may yet live.'

Sudas resisted the urge to smile in response, if only to show his cynicism for Anu's pretentiously generous offer. 'I thought the Anu believe in hunting down their enemy and keeping a bounty on their heads until every last survivor is accounted for.'

Anu spread his hands palm upwards in the universal

gesture of helplessness. 'They will have a headstart and a fair chance to escape.'

Sudas gestured at the lines of cavalry still continuing to line up behind Anu and his companions, then pointed upriver. 'The only way out of Trtsu territory is through your armies. Not one survivor would get through alive and you know this as well as I.'

Anu shrugged and grinned broadly, his teeth flashing white. 'That is my best offer, Sudas, take it or leave it.'

That glimpse of Anu's teeth puzzled Sudas for a moment. Then he saw a flash of reflection off the Anu king's bronze armour and understood. *The light is changing.*

And it was, the air was growing brighter around them. He glanced upwards towards the western sky but the cloud cover was as dense as ever. Perhaps the sun was glancing off the underside of the cloudbank and getting through somehow. Either way, he found that colour was starting to leech back into the world, slowly.

Down below, the river had slowed to a trickle. Barely a brook now, a man could step across it easily. He saw the kings of the Alinas and Bhrigus point and whisper to one another.

'You cannot hope to survive this any other way,' Anu continued, 'At least this way, by surrendering to me and bowing your head to acknowledge me as samrat, you will save your own life and the lives of your wife and children.'

Sudas frowned. 'You would spare me? And spare Sudevi, Indrani and Indraut as well? That is something I never thought I would ever hear an Anu say!'

The Anu did not merely hunt down their enemies after a battle or war; they wiped out their entire families.

Anu smiled again, but this time there were no teeth evident. 'I will spare their lives. You have my word.'

He dipped his chin, his eyes glowing in the waxing light.

Of course. Sudas understood at once. That look said it all.

'You mean you would pass Sudevi around to your new friends to be used as they will. And my children made dasyas.'

Anu made no gesture this time, maintaining his gaze, eyes set intently on Sudas's face.

'At least they will still be alive,' Anu said shortly.

Now, Sudas did smile. 'And what did you have in mind for me, Anu? A dasya too? Or perhaps a lackey to care for your dogs and feed your horses? No, even that would be too good for me, would it not? I am sure you would think of some suitably menial and life-sapping occupation for me to pursue for the rest of my days – few though they might be.'

Anu did not say a word. His gaze stayed fixed on Sudas.

Sudas shook his head slowly. 'I must respectfully decline your offer. I stand with my people to the end. I ask for no clemency nor do I promise it. Whichever of us wins this battle, has the right to do to his enemy all that is permitted by kshatriya dharma. I expect no more and no less than I would mete out to you.'

Anu raised his head at last. He looked around at his fellow kings.

None seemed surprised or even remotely interested in Sudas's response. If anything, they seemed more than a little bored. And at least a half dozen were actually eager to get on with the real task at hand.

Sudas clearly saw the Ajas, Sigrus, Yaksus, Bhrigus and Matsyas grin and look pleased at his answer. *They want the satisfaction of killing me and my kin. Yet only yesterday they sat in my hall and drank and ate and laughed and sang with me.* He felt a touch of sadness at their duplicity. Not betrayed, for the guilt of betrayal was their burden to bear. He had never demanded loyalty, nor was he angered by its absence. Ultimately, a person's dharma was that person's dharma – to uphold or fail to uphold it, was also that person's choice.

'In that case,' Anu said casually, as if proposing to his fellow guests that they proceed to dinner, 'shall we let the festivities begin?'

All ten kings roared in unison. All except the Puru and the Yadus, Sudas noted. They only looked at one another and then at Sudas, then turned their horses' heads and followed the rest of their group.

Anu led the Dasarajna about a half mile away from the riverbank and off to one side, near the start of the woods.

They stopped there, clearly meaning to remain in an observational position while their forces crossed the river and did the actual fighting.

Why should they sully their swords in the first wave? They shall wait until we are decimated and beaten down, then come after their men and finish us off.

It made him bitter, to know that even his fellow kings would not do him the honour of charging against him. As kings against a king, it was expected of them.

But Sudas had no intention of shouting angrily and venting his frustration at them from this distance.

In any case, it would all be over soon. Slain by the swords of ordinary kshatriyas or by the blades of kings, either way he would die on this kusa field today.

But not just yet.

He still had one thing on his side, perhaps the only thing in his favour on this hopeless day.

Strategy.

6

THE LIGHT continued to grow, reaching beacon-like intensity. It filled the world from earth to sky – if not the sky itself then at least to the belly of the brooding cloudbank that hovered ominously over the entire Five Rivers plain. The vast ocean of kusa grass sprang to life once again, brilliant green. Colour leached back into the gentle skirted slopes of Mount Uttunga, turning it leaf green, sala brown and cedar white again, while the summit, high above their heads, towered against the blindingly bright wash that filled the sky. The very cloudbank above seemed ablaze as if a hundred suns were burning above it, their fire seeping through.

The gaudy light illuminated teeth, the whites of eyes, the white anga-vastras worn by the Trtsus, making them seem to glow preternaturally. The polished bronze armour of the ten kings gleamed across the river as well, as did the tin and copper plates of the less elaborate shieldings of the horse brigades of the enemy. The Trtsu had chosen not to use armour and to take up copper arms instead. These shone in the newly reborn light though nowhere near as brightly as the bronze and tin across the river. The endless rows of armoured cavalry made for a river unto itself, a river of metal and pain waiting to come roaring at the Trtsus and end their days. The real river should have glistened silver in this light, but had been the first casualty of the day. Completely extinguished now, even the trickle had ceased, leaving only the bare bed.

Into this empty riverbed, the enemy was dumping great loads of timber. From behind the treeline, elephants had emerged, struggling to haul oversized flatbed carts loaded with logs of timber. Sudas guessed that these were part of the timber excavated from the northern foothills, near the damworks. The reason why the enemy had hauled them all the way downriver to this point was obvious.

The timber logs were enormous in length and thickness and perfectly fit the riverbed's depth and width at this point. Farther upriver, the logs would not reach across the bed. But over here, they were perfect.

After the first wave of elephants had unloaded their burdens, and teams of labourers, overseen by military foremen who guided them in placing the logs across its span had finished their work of tying the logs together, the result was quite impressive. A veritable bridge now spanned the empty riverbed. Testing the result by sending a pair of men across on foot, the foremen watched as the two labourers crossed to the Trtsu side, gazed insolently at Sudas and his horsemen, then turned and walked back. A loud succession of cheers rose from the enemy lines, followed by loud trumpeting cries from the elephants who were being rewarded for their vital part in the operation.

Bolan was right; this operation has been in progress for at least a year. This was to be a carefully planned and executed takeover of Trtsu territories.

There now stood a bridge across the Parusni four score yards wide. Enough for an army to cross. Sudas watched as various parts of the bridge were tested further, by horsemen, then by elephants, and marvelled at the sheer scale of engineering and planning. *Bravo,* he thought without bitterness or acrimony. *This is Bharata genius at its best. Now, if only we could use this same genius to live and work together instead of warring constantly, we would be able to bring peace and prosperity and civilisation to the entire known world.*

Ucchasrava returned as the last test was completed, and the elephant turned around with some difficulty after having reached the Trtsu side. The animal appeared to want to come towards Trtsu land rather than turn back, no doubt attracted by the vast field of kusa before him. This was elephant swargaloka right here. The mahout cursed and prodded and cajoled as horsemen barred the pachyderm's way by waving pointed spears.

'Rajan,' Ucchas said, sweat running down his face in twin runnels.

The clammy dullness of the air had changed in the past hour, giving way to a humid miasma. Sudas did not understand the vagaries of weather well enough to know what that meant but he seemed to recall it had something to do with impending rain or thunderstorms. Wet palms before thunderstorms, was it? Or dry palms? He shook his head, focussing on his lieutenant's report.

'It is as we feared, they have the river as far as the eye can see,' Ucchas said. He swept his palm across his forehead, wiping off the sweat. 'Their numbers are hard to make out beyond the line of trees – they have used the tree cover to conceal their elephants and what appears to be siege machinery.'

'Not siege machinery,' Drahkyu corrected, 'Bridge material.' He gestured towards the river.

Ucchas saw the timber spanning the breadth of the river for the first time and started. 'Blessed Mitra and Varuna! They will be across in no time now.'

'How many horses?' Sudas asked.

Ucchas shook his head, wiping off the sweat which was draining off his neck now. The others were sweating too and even Sudas could feel tiny beads crowding his hairline now; his growing anxiety manifesting itself in this rather visible form. Sudevi always teased him about sweating so much from the crown. *Because your brain works as hard as your body.* 'Fifty score company, perhaps hundred score, perhaps even more. The ranks continue upriver as far as the eye...'

'...can see, yes,' Sudas interjected. 'What colour is their armour?'

Ucchas blinked. 'Their krtadhvaj are in numerous colours. The Anu carry saffron and white, the Bhrigu...'

Sudas slapped his thigh impatiently. 'Not their banners, man! Their armour! Is it tin, copper, bronze... iron?'

'Iron?' Atharva repeated, startled. Sweat was pouring down him like on a pig in fever, Sudas noted. How long would he last at this rate? But he did not have the heart to tell him to retire, not now. 'Nobody can work iron into armour. Nobody can work iron into more than a blob or brick! Don't dream up more nightmares, we already have enough to deal with, Rajan!' Sudas nodded, speaking more kindly to the sick young man. It was clear that even if Atharva survived the battle, the fever would not let him last beyond the night. No man could ride and fight with such heat searing his brain and hope to survive more than a few hours.

'I know it, we all know it. Yet more things have happened today than we all dreamed possible. Iron exists, and someday humankind will possess the tools and wherewithal to be able to work it into weapons, armour and shields.'

'Even so,' Thsang said skeptically, 'it is too heavy to carry! What use would it serve? Iron is a useless metal, every forgeman knows that. Too hard to work with and too heavy to make efficient arms or armour. We may as well use lead!'

Sudas ignored Thsang's comments and looked at Ucchas. 'I do not wish to waste time arguing about this. I only wish to know what kind of armour the enemy are decked out in.'

Ucchas nodded. 'Tin mostly, from the silvery reflection. Their lieutenants have a mixture of copper and tin. Only the kings possess the full bronze armour, shields and weapons.'

Sudas looked out across the river, then allowed himself a grin. 'Very well then. Indra is on our side.'

'What do you mean, Rajan?' asked one of the others – Daha, from the voice. 'How does it matter what armour or weapons they use?'

Sudas did not turn to look at the man. He was busy looking at the river. The mahout and horsemen had finally succeeded in persuading the stubborn elephant to turn and return to its herd. From the movement in the cavalry lines, he guessed that they would start to cross in moments, and launch the first wave of attack. It was time.

'You shall see,' he said. 'Now I want each of you to repeat once more what his role in the battle shall be. Everyone must work together if we are to achieve our goal. Let us go over my instructions once again.'

7

'STEADY!' SUDAS called loudly.

Ucchas and the other lieutenants passed on the command, steadying the lone ragged line of Trtsu.

The first regiment of enemy cavalry had completed their crossing and were lining up along the Trtsu side of the river now. Their frontline stretched as wide as the Trtsu except that they had three men for every Trtsu. These were daunting but not impossible odds. Sudas had been a little concerned that the enemy might throw everything at them from the get-go, but apparently Anu's word still prevailed over the ten kings. This regiment was made up solely of Anu horsemen, as was evident from the saffron and white krtadhvaj flapping from the poles. It was what he had hoped for. Anu smelled a sure victory and wanted to snatch all the glory for himself. The remaining nine kings would have to be content with picking at the remains in his wake.

Sudas watched as the Anu lieutenants ordered their companies to straighten their lines.

'Ready for my command,' Sudas called out.

Again, the order was relayed to either side. He was fore and centre, his lieutenants placed every half-score men or so apart, to ensure that communication was maintained effectively and the plan was followed exactly as outlined. Now the time for strategising was past. It was time to put into action everything he had planned and prepared for. To attempt boldly to snatch honour from the jaws of defeat. Not victory, perhaps, for that would be asking too much of the gods. But honour itself was a noble prize. And he would have settled for honour were he an ordinary man, or only a kshatriya, a Trtsu, or a Bharata. But as a king, he needed to do much more. A king needed to win. Losing, however honourably, was not an option.

The Anu cavalry drew their swords. Anu favoured the use of long swords even for horse combat. Neither spears nor lances for them, nor did they use javelins. The Anu horse cavalry was a proud one, flushed with more victories than any other Bharata tribe. *That is mainly because they go to war more than any other Bharata tribe, and almost always a war of their choosing, fought at a time, place and under circumstances that are in their favour.* But he was glad to see that they were adhering to norm. After the numerous surprises and shocks of the day, he had feared that perhaps even these certainties might prove to be ungrounded. His plan depended on certain constants. Without sure knowledge, no plan could be effective. The heavier the rock to be thrown, the firmer the ground the thrower must stand upon.

'Anu!' cried the enemy with one voice as they charged.

'Jai Bharata!' came the Trtsu response, bracing for the attack, although they did not draw their own weapons.

'Steady!'

Sudas cried out as the Anu cavalry started forward with an impressively disciplined trot, which built to a canter, and then broke into a gallop. The Trtsu had fallen back to the edge of the kusa sea, barely half a mile from the riverbank. The Anu were eating up the ground in moments.

Sudas watched as the Anu roared closer, swords and

armour gleaming brightly in the evening sun. The sun shone through holes in the cloudbank as it had done that morning when he had watched from the peak of Uttunga, casting great swatches of brightness and shadow on the plains. The Anu galloped from a patch of sunshine, their metalwork shining, into a shadow patch, where they suddenly turned dull and grey.

He could see the whites of their eyes now, and their bared teeth. They were enjoying this charge. The Trtsu might be their brethren, but they were also the stronger of the two tribes; the Anu were clearly relishing the opportunity to smack their stronger brother's head into the ground. *And lop it off*, Sudas thought grimly. He had respect for the charging horsemen as fellow Bharatas, fellow kshatriyas, even fellow humans. But to use their swords and strength in an unjust war was not honourable. They were betraying their dharma and their humanity by undertaking this campaign, and they were doing so vindictively and viciously. That was not the Arya way, nor the Bharata way. It made what he and his men were about to do that much easier – he could dole out justice without remorse or mercy now.

The Anu were barely a score yards away, close enough for him to see the hair on their beards and count how many good teeth each man had left in his grinning mouth. These were the youngest and best of their yoddhas, not a grey hair among the lot. Sudas could see powerful muscles rippling through the gaps in the armour plates, which had been left in order to permit the wearer free movement in a swordfight and while riding. Even the horses were battle veterans, with their white eyes and shiny snouts, which could smell the excitement and thrill of imminent slaughter.

'Turn!' Sudas cried suddenly, and did as he himself bid, twisting Saryu's reins and nudging her with both knees. He leaped forward, and in a few steps, was inside the kusa field. To either side of him, his men did the same, riding as hard as the Anu, but *away* from them.

The entire Trtsu line turned with Sudas and lost itself in the sea of kusa. Silently, they dispersed as they had been ordered, guided with spoken commands by their lieutenants. The grass rippled as they galloped deeper into the field with the tall, wavering stalks closing in around them, concealing them as effectively as a veil conceals a woman.

The Anu screamed in outrage.

Sudas heard them as he rode, darting one score

yards west, then cutting sharply east, then north and east, then sharply turning northwest, proscribing a zigzag path that would be impossible to follow.

He was perhaps four score yards into the kusa when he heard the shouts of outrage and confusion among the Anu and the whinnying of charging horses that had been pulled to an abrupt halt.

He grinned, able to see the chaos in his mind's eye as clearly as if he were present among them.

The Anu had been expecting the Trtsu to make one last stubborn stand. They had thought they would face the charge and fight as best as they could, battling until they were wiped out to the last man or boy. After that, they planned to signal the rest of the force, so that the Ten Kings could cross over in triumph, and the army could scour Trtsu lands, seeking out, hunting down, and slaughtering every last Trtsu elder, young'un, woman and girl, until no one was left alive.

They had not been expecting the Trtsu frontline to turn tail and flee into the kusa grass without a single sword raised.

'Craven!' called the frustrated cavalry. 'Trtsu cowards!' There were many more unmentionable terms and epithets hurled by the Anu regiment, milling about in the dust and confusion. Horses cried out in disappointment.

Sudas grinned. The insults did not trouble him. This was not cowardice because they were not running away from the battle, merely changing the field to suit their advantage. Besides, with such overwhelming numbers pitted against them, they were entitled to respond with strategic and tactical methods.

He slowed his horse, then slipped off and led her on further through the grass a half score yards before slapping her on the rump and chasing her further into the kusa. She was wise and obedient enough to know that she was expected to stay there. Besides, the ample supply of fresh delicious grass was a cornucopia for any equine. All through the kusa his Trtsu were doing the same with their horses, dismounting, sending their mounts further inland, and then doubling back.

To the Anu, it appeared as if the Trtsu, their heads visible above the tips of the stalks until now, had suddenly vanished from sight.

Moving as one man, Sudas and his men through the kusa sea, back towards the enemy. The Anu wanted a fight and they would get one, but on Trtsu terms.

8

THE WIND which had been absent all day now returned. Like a sigh from an awakened god, it kissed the tips of the kusa stalks, rippling through the vast undulating fields. Sudas felt that first kiss of wind on his sweating scalp and took it as a benediction from Vayu. Then the wind grew in strength and speed until the kusa was dancing again as it had been that morning. He felt curiously refreshed and invigorated.

He took up his bow and waited for a target. He knew the other Trtsus were doing the same.

The Anu had made the dangerous error of entering the kusa sea on horseback. To their minds, it must have seemed logical – the height would give them a better view and a tactical advantage. It did both those things.

But it also made them more easily visible to the Trtsu.

On foot in the tall grass, effectively hidden from view, barely a score yards away, the Trtsu could simply stand still and wait for the riders to approach within sight and shot.

Sudas could feel the ground beneath his feet vibrating with the hooves of fifty score Anu riding through the fields. He could see the Anu lieutenants in his mind's eye, urging their men onwards, keeping a rigid frontline with a horseman every few yards. They expected to roll over the Trtsus, cut them down as they appeared in the grass, or chase them out of the kusa sea to the open grounds beyond.

Immense as the sea of kusa was, the Anu had a thousand men on horses, riding in waves perhaps ten score wide. They could theoretically sweep the kusa and pick it clean of Trtsus, just as a mother might use a bone comb to sweep out lice from her child's long hair.

But the Trtsus were not lice.

Sudas felt the approaching hooves draw closer through the vibrations in the soles of his feet long before he actually saw the heads of the horsemen. When they came into sight, it was the gleaming tips of their helmets that first grew visible through the stalks. Those tips caught the evening sunlight and reflected it beautifully. He could see well enough to aim at the approaching helmets when they were still three score yards away. He sent up a silent prayer of thanks to Surya, the sun god, for marking out his targets so well.

What was more, the wind was behind him. That meant he would be shooting with Vayu's hand guiding his aim, not against the god of wind.

He aimed at the gleaming helmets bobbing slowly as they approached, and then lowered his aim just a mite. Striking that chest armour at this range, he might or might not have been able to punch through with a shortbow, which was what all Trtsu carried when riding. But because he had devised this strategy, he had armed his men accordingly. The bow in Sudas's hands was not a shortbow, but a full longbow, with a string pressure capable of sending a bolt that could pierce a tin plate, copper, and even bronze if shot from close.

The Anu cavalry were armoured in tin. Only the lieutenants had copperplate.

He loosed the first arrow.

And heard the distinctive sound of an arrowhead pierceing through metalplate – tin plate in particular made a unique hollow echoing sound – followed by a wet cry from the man who had been hit.

His second arrow was strung before he heard the sound of the man's body hitting the ground.

He loosed again, and this time heard no metal clamour, just the death rattle of a man struck in the throat.

A third arrow. Loose again.

Metal clank. A cry.

Shouts along the Anu line. More metallic sounds. More cries. More bodies falling to the ground. Horses whinnying in alarm.

The Trtsus were letting loose.

For the next several minutes, Sudas aimed and shot until the tips of his fingers burned as if he had held them over an open flame.

He had loosed a score of arrows.

Every single one had hit its mark, although he thought that two of the men might have received non-fatal wounds and at least one had still stayed on his horse.

Time to move on.

He ran through the kusa, using the same technique he had used that morning – the same that all Trtsu children used when playing 'hide and seek' in the grass.

After zigzagging for several moments, he took up

a new position and resumed his attack.

He loosed another score of arrows, although this time round he struck the mark only half the time. The Anu had begun watching for arrows and were deflecting them with their shields and swords. They may have been outmaneuvered, but they were not stupid. They had recovered quickly enough and were rallying. He also heard excited shouts and the sound of horses rearing and thumping down again and knew that some of his Trtsus were being fished out and killed. Hard as it was to spot his people, once spotted, killing them was easy. He guessed that some of the Anu had dismounted for precisely this purpose, and that the enemy was now proceeding with mounted soldiers as well as those on foot. The Anu lieutenants were battle-smart after all. They had adapted to the situation fairly quickly.

Even so, the Trtsus had the tactical advantage. And each man had been allotted four score arrows, the maximum number that could easily be carried by a single man.

Sudas made use of every single one of them. When the last arrow left his string, striking home with an unmistakable cry from an Anu throat, he felt content. The first part of his strategy had worked well. The aim had been to survive the first hour of battle and to make the enemy suffer maximum casualties while retaining most if not all of his own force.

He had no way of knowing how many men had fallen on either side, but he knew that the Anu losses had been considerable. He was fairly certain that he alone had been responsible for the slaughter of no less than one-and-a-half score Anu, and wounded another score. Thirty dead, twenty wounded, by a single man. Even if every Trtsu had fared perhaps half as well as he had – although he knew that some were equally good or better bowmen than he – that would still account for a prodigious number of fallen enemy soldiers. He could hope that twenty score or more Anu lay dead or severely wounded in the kusa now. By the time of his last position shift, he had begun passing armoured bodies fallen in the grass, even a horse or two, and sadly, one Trtsu corpse, hacked beyond recognition by a dozen swords.

It was time to move on to the next part of his plan.

He glanced at the western sky. The sun, now peering through the clouds more frequently than it had all day, was perhaps two hours from setting. That was one advantage of the Dasarajna battle taking place on one of the longest days of the year, but under the circumstances, even two hours could be too long for a force as small as his own to hold out against an army that large.

He fell back, racing away from the river, circling around towards the thicket at the bottom of Uttunga, the same spot where he had instructed Indrani and Indraut to wait for him that morning.

Several of his Trtsus were already there, crouched or seated on the ground, recovering from battle. They were all stained green with the grass and soaked wet by the omnipresent dew. The horses were starting to drift in pairs and threes, following the trail of Saryu who was standing proudly beneath the peepal tree where Sudas always left her, flicking her tail. She whickered softly with pleasure when he came up to her, and he kissed her on the side of her snout. She nudged his neck with her snout, telling him she was glad he was still alive.

Sudas collapsed to the ground, allowing himself a few moments to recover. Suddenly a shadow fell across him and he looked up, expecting to see one of his lieutenants. But it was not one of his men.

9

Sudevi fell to her knees and embraced Sudas, kissing his face and showering more kisses on his neck and arms, not caring about the grass stains or dirt or sweat.

'You were supposed to be on the summit,' he said accusingly, but without reproach. He was glad for her touch. It was always necessary to remember what one was fighting and killing for.

'I was,' she said. 'I could see everything. We all could but the others were working tooth and nail to finish Guru Vashishta's chore. The children and I were keeping a lookout and we saw everything.'

'And?' he asked.

She took his face in her hands. 'Your battle in the kusa fields was a great success. You know this already, do you not?'

He shrugged. 'I could barely see five yards beyond my own face. I only know what I could hear or catch a glimpse of.' She laughed, showing her throat, the lovely curves of her smooth neck. Her hair was drawn up and tied to the right and like him and the rest of his soldiers, she was also clad in white.

'You should have seen it! I counted thirty score dead and another five score who will not last out the night. The Anu are still striving to find their wounded and account for their dead in the grass. They scurry about like ants in a fire!'

'Thirty score dead,' he said wonderingly. 'Six hundred? Maybe more? Are you certain?'

She laughed again. 'I am positive, my love. They were routed! You wiped out an entire regiment of the finest Anu yoddhas with barely two hundred men and boys! My half-brother will never bear the humiliation!'

Sudas nodded slowly. 'He will be raging and ranting. Now he must ride into battle himself and take charge of the next attack. He will need to prove himself before his fellow kings and regain his lost honour. He will be angry and eager to crush us quickly and decisively.'

Sudevi stopped smiling. 'Anu can be terrible when

he is angry and at war. I have heard of and seen his cruelties.'

Sudas put a hand on her shoulder, touching her throat with his fingertips. Still sore from the bowstring, the soft skin of her neck felt soothing to his touch. 'That is good. It is exactly what we want.'

'You want Anu to be angry? To crush you with his cruelty?'

'I want him to be emotionally driven and unable to think rationally.'

She shook her head. 'He is not a fool, Sudas. He is a brilliant tactician.'

'But a bad strategist.'

She frowned. 'What is the difference? Aren't they the same thing, strategy and tactics?'

'Not quite. Anu is good at knowing which force to send in at a particular point in a battle and how to organise operations during the fight. But his weakness has always been that he is unable to plan a campaign in advance and prepare for it beforehand. The first is tactics, the second is strategy.'

She gestured westwards, in the direction of the Parusni. 'From the sight of all that preparation and the timberworks, not to mention the organising of the alliance of ten kings, the readiness of their armies, the fact that he was able to move such a huge force so close so quickly, and had thought out every step of the operation, right from the damworks to the bridgeworks, display very astute strategic planning.'

Sudas looked at her a long moment, then smiled slowly. 'It is. But it is not a new strategy, nor is it original to Anu's mind.'

'I don't understand.'

'These things he has done, they are what anyone would have done were they to attempt to seize Trtsu lands. One of the most important lessons I learned about strategy was being able to predict the strategy of one's attackers, especially when in a defencive position and holding a fixed garrison. You study your own weaknesses, geographical as well as human ones, and think about how a potential enemy would come at you. Since geography and human limitations are more or less fixed, it is possible to estimate what any invader's future plan is likely to be and prepare for it.'

She frowned. 'Prepare for it? So you suspected that Anu would dam the river, breach the banks, and ally with the other kings to launch this assault today?'

'Not today, but someday, possibly. I hoped it

would never happen. But in the event it did, I had to be prepared.'

'And you are? Prepared?'

'As best as one can be against superior odds and numbers. We have geography aiding us, as you saw during the battle in the grass. And we have the weather on our side as well.'

'The weather?'

He smiled and stroked her cheek. 'That is what Guru Vashishta says. He feels this is the perfect day for this battle. So perfect, that he feels that it is a sign that Indra, Varuna and Vayu are on our side in this fray.'

'I should hope so. We need all the help we can get.' She paused. 'Is that what Guru Vashishta's task is for? Is it somehow related to your strategy for this battle?'

'If all goes well,' Sudas replied. 'I must warn you though. No matter how effective a counter-strategy, and no matter how well the day goes for us today, we are beaten down by the sheer force of numbers. I could never have expected such a complete betrayal of our allies and friends. Two or three kings, surely, even five or six perhaps. But ten kings? And individual rovers and freeholders? Look at the size of that army out there! It is beyond the realm of possibility that we will win the day. I fight only for the sake of honour and because it is my dharma to fight until the last breath. I do not say we will lose but that we are likely to die fighting for victory.'

She looked at him. Her eyes were shiny and wet with tears, but he saw that they were tears of happiness and possibly hope. She kissed him again, fiercely, and he felt her hot tears on his own cheek. 'I shall pray to the devas you succeed in every last detail,' she said. 'And I shall raise my own sword and fight alongside you before this day ends.'

She put a finger upon his lips before he could protest. 'I will brook no argument over it, Sudas. I am a Bharata too now, and mother to the future king and queen of the Bharata nation. That makes me the queen mother, I think,' she laughed, 'Or some such! In any case, I am no sweet-scented Anu concubine to lie on my silks and wait for the victor to come possess me. I am a Bharata woman and a Trtsu queen and I shall fight alongside my husband and my fellow citizens, regardless of the outcome of this battle.'

He removed her fingers from his lips, kissed them, and then said, 'You shall do as you wish. That freedom of choice is one of the very things we are fighting to uphold in this conflict. I may not like the idea of you putting yourself in harm's way, but I respect it and shall uphold your right.'

He looked around. A sizable crowd had collected by now. He was heartened by the numbers. It appeared as if a majority of his men had survived the battle in the grass. All his lieutenants were present as well, except for the ones who were still occupied with helping Guru Vashishta. And Atharva. He could not see Atharva anywhere.

Had the poor young man succumbed to his fever then?

He saw Ucchasrava and beckoned him. At once, the other Trtsus began to form up and seat themselves cross-legged on the ground around him, like shishyas around a guru at a gurukul.

'What is the tally?' he asked Ucchas.

Ucchas grinned. 'It is very good, Rajan. We lost only a few score, and about half that number came back with wounds and injuries.'

Alena added: 'One died of snakebite. Poor fellow.'

Sudas was pleased too but did not smile. 'We shall grieve for the fallen later. Right now, we move ahead as planned. We shall first—'

He was interrupted by shouts from a familiar pair of young throats. He looked up, mortified to see Indrani and Indraut come racing down from the path that led up to the base point of Uttunga, the same way they had descended that morning.

'Pitr!' Indrani shouted, reaching him first, out of breath and covered with dust from her rapid descent. 'The enemy has crossed the river and is attacking again in full force.'

'We saw it from the summit, Pitr,' Indraut added as he came up, also panting. 'They are sweeping across the whole plain. One entire regiment is heading this way. That is why we had to disobey Maatr's order and come down at once. We saw them as we were at base point. They were only a mile away at the time. They will be here in moments!'

10

Sudas rode his horse hard. Saryu was glad for the exercise. Despite the upheavals of the day, she had not really been tested yet. Now, she had an opportunity to show her mettle. She made the most of it, setting a pace for the others to follow. Sudas had no need to look back. As a Trtsu Bharata he could tell from the sound and vibration of the earth the rough number of horse riders with him, and those following.

Less than ten score of us, with over fifty score following.

The odds were the same as they had faced in the kusa grass. But this time they were on open ground and the enemy was in pursuit. Had they stood and fought, it would have been a massacre. The enemy had thousands more already on this side of the river, with the rest crossing over in quick succession. Anu and his allies were taking no chances this time, they were throwing everything they had at the Trtsu, in a bid to annihilate them quickly, with minimal losses. It was the right thing to do – in a sense, the *only* thing. He would have done the same had the situation been reversed. That was why, as he had explained to Sudevi earlier, he had been expecting it.

Still, Anu was truly baying for blood. He was riding his horses harder than he ought to, with their heavy armoured riders. Then again, Sudas mused grimly as he bent low over the reins, Anu knew that he did not need to chase them for very long. He had no fear of tiring out his horses.

Anu was right about one thing – the chase would be a short, fierce one.

Already, Sudas could see the rice and wheat fields to the east appear ahead, pleasing in their symmetry, extending for yojanas in that direction. These were the real treasures of the Trtsu territories, the precious alluvial river plains that yielded the finest harvests in the world. Whatever one wished to grow, could be grown here, in this land of Five Rivers. There was already enough grain in the fields to feed all the ten nations who were warring against them today. Thousands upon thousands of quintals of grain, waiting to be harvested. Ever since the roving gramas had decided to discontinue their nomadic ways and settle down in one place, taking to cattle herding and crop raising in place of hunting and foraging, no place more suitable for human inhabitation or more bountiful in harvest had been found by the tribes. This was truly a land worth fighting for.

He guided Saryu around the foot of Uttunga, keeping her head turned south as they came around the gently circling natural curve of the land.

He did not wish to ride east into those crop fields. There was nothing but three score miles of food there, and no place to hide or fight. Besides, he had no wish to destroy the crop they had worked so hard on, if he could help it. His destination lay to the south of Uttunga itself.

He smiled into the wind as he rubbed his cheek against Saryu's neck and mane.

What must Anu be thinking now that he must have realised that Sudas was leading them around the mountain, back to the south bank of the Parusni?

He would be thinking that Sudas had lost his senses, to be leading his meagre force back towards the very spot where the invaders were crossing the riverbed!

Sudevi was not far behind him, to his right. Between her and Sudas were Indrani and Indraut, riding admirably well again, as they had that morning.

He glanced over at them and felt a twinge of unease. If only they had stayed on the summit. He had sent all three of them there to be safe from these first stages of the battle, when almost anything could go wrong. Now here they were, in the thick of harm's way. There was little he could do to protect them, when he was already struggling against impossible odds.

They were in the eastern shadow of Mount Uttunga now. It was much darker here than on the western side, because the mountain blocked the evening sun. He could see the shadow stretching out to his left for what seemed like a mile. That told him how low the sun was already – less than two hours before sundown. Not much time left, if Guru Vashishta's calculations were correct. The storm would strike just after sunset, the guru had said, and that marked the final phase of their plan.

There was still a great deal to be done though, before that happened, not just by the Trtsus but by the enemy. For the plan depended on the enemy following a certain strategy as well as responding in a certain way to Sudas's counter-strategy.

This game was similar to the ones they played with bone dice on a wooden board; the only difference was that here their stones were living breathing men, who would be killed if he took the wrong decisions or actions. And three of the stones on the board represented the three persons who were most beloved to him.

He felt the ground curve beneath Saryu's hooves again, turning as the mountain's lowermost extremities curved as well. He kept the mare's head turning just enough so that she followed the curve of the mountain while still running in as straight a line as possible. Trees, bushes, boulders, everything whipped past, mere blurs as he sped along. He hoped the other horses were as fit and in as good fettle as his own.

He looked over his shoulder and then regretted having done so.

It was no good looking back, the dust of his own riders formed too thick a cloud to be able to see the pursuers.

But he knew they were there, close on their heels. He could almost see Anu's face, swathed in swirls of dust from the Trtsus ahead, thin lips pursed in an expression of cold fury. He would be swearing he would kill each Trtsu twice in order to make up for all the good men he had lost.

Sudas came around the gentle undulating curve of Uttunga and finally saw the Parusni reappear ahead. It was unnerving to see the river bed, so brown and bone dry. He thought of all the river life that must have died downstream from the dam. He had seen fish flopping about and larger creatures gasping as they died at the main crossing point, but for some reason only now did he realise how many of those acquatic creatures must have been killed by the man-made dam. They too were casualties of Anu's greed and the lust of the Ten Kings.

He tried to spy the crossing point but the roughly circular base of Uttunga was a very wide circle, and the crossing point was still a whole mile to the west.

He was relieved to see that none of the enemy forces were coming around this way to cut them off. The Anu had given chase probably expecting them to race back to the city. Any messengers they might have sent back to their allies would not have reached them yet with the word that, in fact, the Trtsus were merely circling around the mountain.

Besides, if they continued this way, they would meet up with the enemy in any case, so why divert more forces in this direction? Anu wanted to chase them down and slaughter them himself.

That was what Sudas had been counting on.

He saw the pre-arranged mark up ahead, a great boulder the size of his great hall, with its southern face shaped somewhat like a man's profile. That was the Prince, called so by the Trtsus, for it appeared as though a royal were standing and surveying his vast kingdom extending across the river and forests.

He came around the face of the Prince, then turned Saryu sharply, ducking down as low-hanging trees rushed at him. He knew the others would follow his example – even Sudevi and his children, who did not know this stage of his plan. After riding about five score yards under the low-hanging branches, he passed through a narrow rock funnel, and emerged into an open space with the sky visible above as a long grey strip, and the looming shape of Uttunga directly above.

Sudevi was close on his heels, along with Indrani, Indraut, Daha, Bolan and Alena. The rest of his lieutenants were bringing up the rear, making sure that none of the Trtsus missed the rendezvous point and that the Anu took the bait. Sudas knew that Drahkyu and Daha would likely be shooting arrows backwards at the Anu as they rode, for they were experts at doing anything on a horse, while Atharva and Alena would ride on the eastern flank and make sure nobody got left behind.

'Here!' Sudas shouted, dismounting by one of the walls of the box canyon and unfolding the large bundle carefully wrapped in oiled furs to keep it safe in the event of rain. 'Take these in place of your present weapons! Quickly! Pass them on!'

Sudevi took one of the weapons he was handing out rapidly, all but throwing them at his men as they crowded close. She reacted to the weight and the look of the unusual sword.

'What is this?' she cried out above the noise, for the box canyon multiplied the sounds of the horse's hooves and men's shouts. Dust rose in a cloud, obscuring their vision too.

'Iron,' Sudas told her with a grim smile. 'Weapons tooled from solid iron and worked as thin as possible.'

She stared at the roughly shaped sword, ugly and inelegant compared to their beautifully tooled bronze swords with carved inlays and jewelled hilts. 'How ugly! Is it any use?'

Sudas grinned. 'Wait and see.'

Ucchas came up, taking a large hacking blade with a two-handed grip – even Sudas was not sure what one called such a weapon. A sword-axe? 'They are almost here. Mitra! This is heavy!'

Sudas clapped a hand on his lieutenant's shoulder. 'It is worth its weight, I can assure you!'

Sudas waited a moment to let some of the dust and noise subside. Alena and Drahkyu had wisely moved the horses to the back of the canyon, to give the Trtsu fighting space. Sudevi took Indrani and Indraut and took up a position beyond the horses, calming them as well as putting further distance between the children and the fighting that would break out in moments.

Sudas raised his own sword high to attract his men's attention and called out loudly,

'Swing these with all the force you can muster. Remember what Guru Vashishta told us! Trust the metal to do its job!'

They nodded, but he could see them exchange nervous glances. None of them had actually fought a battle with weapons made from iron before. Many were still superstitious about the use of the metal, believing it was a symbol of Kali, the dreaded dark king who was fated to rule the last age of itihasa, the eponymous Age of Kali. Others wondered what was wrong with good old copper, tin and brass that they should be discarded for these rough and unaesthetic brutes.

Indra, be with us, Sudas prayed silently, then turned to face the mouth of the canyon's entrance.

11

'SUDAS!' CRIED the familiar voice of Anu from outside the overhang. 'I know you are in there. Come out and fight like men!'

'Anu,' Sudas replied calmly. 'We have no place to go from here. This is our last stand. If you have courage enough to face a cornered lion, then come in and feel our final cut.'

There were several rounds of curses and shouts from Anu's ranks, followed by a loud and angry discussion that ended abruptly. Sudas heard the clink of tin and copper armour along with a succession of other sturdier thuds.

The Anu were dismounting and coming towards them on foot.

The trap was sprung.

He looked back at his men. Here, at the mouth

of the canyon's entrance, the distance from one side of the rock to the other was less than six yards. Sufficient width for two or three men to cover at a time. It was the reason he had chosen this site – when faced with larger numbers, one had to find a way to restrict the approach of enemy troops. This way, the Anu's superior force was negated. They might number in thousands, but they would still be able to enter the canyon only three at a time. Any more than that and they risked harming one another in a sword fight at such close quarters. And when they did enter, Sudas's men were waiting to slaughter them with their heavy iron swords.

Sudas beckoned to Ucchas and Bolan. They seemed the freshest of all the Trtsus. 'We three shall take the first round,' he said. 'The rest shall stay behind, just inside the mouth of the canyon. If any of us falls, only one must take his place. At any time, let there be no more than three of us here. Understood?'

Heads bobbed.

Atharva pushed forward, holding an iron weapon in one hand and a copper sword in the other. Sudas's heart leaped, seeing him still alive and standing. It was clear that the young warrior accomplished both feats with considerable difficulty. His face had the sallow complexion that followed a night of high fever. His eyes were hollow pits in his face. It pained Sudas to see him in such a condition.

'Let me stand first, Rajan,' Atharva said, his determination belying his condition. Sudas was about to argue but changed his mind. While an honourable death might not be enough for a king, it was a warrior's chief ambition.

He looked at Ucchas and nodded his head. Ucchas yielded his spot to Atharva and dropped back several yards, staying in the narrow passageway that formed a kind of neck to the canyon. From this mouth six yards wide, the neck reduced by about a yard's width before opening out into the canyon proper. Ucchas stood guarding the neck, positioning others behind him in a chain. It was an adaptation of Sudas's instructions but a good one. That was why good lieutenants were so crucial for the execution of strategies. Conditions on the field of battle always called for adjustments and rearrangements. Sudas was glad he had such good men he could rely on.

He heard the sound of heavy footsteps approaching. The Anu liked to weigh themselves down with as much metal as possible and let their horses carry the burden.

It made them formidable in battle during a mounted cavalry charge, but on the ground, that much armour could also be a hindrance.

Still, Sudas reminded himself that he must not underestimate the enemy. They were fierce warriors; one slip of his plan and all would be lost. The Anu could afford to lose many and still win the day. To the Trtsus, every man counted. And they had only one king for the other ten! Anu himself was not among the first group of men that came down the canyon path. Sudas was disappointed at that – he had hoped the fellow Bharata's anger at being outwitted earlier would have made him careless enough to head the line of attack. But apparently the king of the Anu was thinking tactically. Until he knew what to expect, he was not risking his own neck.

It was a wise choice.

The half score of Anu who came around the last turn looked nonplussed at the sight of only three Trtsus waiting for them.

'Where is the rest of your army?' asked an Anu bedecked in shiny filigreed copper and tin armour and carrying a bronze sword. 'Skulking in a corner?'

Sudas hefted the sword. He liked the extra weight

and the knowledge of what it would do to the enemy when used correctly. 'We are enough to take you on. Each Trtsu is worth a hundred Anu. Or were you not present at the battle in the grass?'

At the mention of the grass, the Anu's smile vanished. No more words were spoken.

Five or six of the Anu came rushing down the path with weapons drawn, roaring loudly. Those behind them roared as well to cheer their fellows on, ready to follow them and commence the slaughter they expected.

Sudas stepped out, turning into the swinging sword of an Anu soldier. He hacked at the man's bronze sword with his iron one. The bronze sword snapped with a peculiar metallic sound, and his iron sword slicked past, catching the man in his midriff. It cleaved through his armour, siniking into his flesh with ease, giving him a brutal fatal wound. Sudas pulled his sword free and gore splattered across the dirt of the path. He turned and met the thrusting point of the next man's sword with a chopping motion that bent the weapon back on itself. The man stopped in his tracks, staring at the distorted metal in his hand with disbelief, and then pulled out his dagger with a roar. Sudas came at him, brandishing his sword, and in one sweeping motion nearly decapitated him. His superior weapon cut through the hilt of the dagger too, slicing it as easily as it cut through flesh. He rammed the point of the sword into the middle of a third man, piercing his armour with a screeching sound. The man bent over Sudas's blade, staring down at the object of his demise.

Sudas pulled the sword free and turned to face the next man.

Beside him, he sensed Atharva and Bolan fighting with equal ease. Blood spurted in great tracks, bodies were dismembered and bones and armour cracked under the relentless onslaught of the iron swords.

It was not so much a question of skill, Sudas mused as he fought on, but that the enemy was unable to parry or counter his blows. Had he been using copper, or even bronze swords, they would have been able to block and deflect his swings and thrusts and retaliate. It would have been an equal fight. Now, nothing they did mattered: The iron weapons cut through their armour and blades as easily as flesh. And because of the sheer weight of the iron blades, any blow that landed on a person was fatal. The only way they could avoid being maimed or killed was to avoid being struck at all, which was nearly impossible at such close quarters.

The tenth or eleventh man who came at Sudas tried to dodge and leap aside to avoid being struck, his sword a truncated half-length of useless metal in his fist. Sudas simply stepped back and waited for the man to come at him. The man glanced back at his waiting comrades, all waiting their turn, and Sudas saw the knowledge in his eyes: He cannot retreat; he will be branded a coward forever. The man turned and came running straight at Sudas. All Sudas had to do was hold out his sword. The man all but impaled himself on it.

After nearly two score men lay dying at the mouth of the canyon entrance, the Anu began to get a sense that something was wrong. Word must have filtered back to Anu himself.

The king appeared soon after, moving aside his men to see for himself if the bizarre rumour was true.

'Iron?' He shouted at Sudas. 'Does your necromancer wizard seek to deceive my men with his childish illusions? Nobody can work iron into usable weapons. And even if they are made, they are useless in combat.'

Sudas chuckled richly as he dispatched yet another

braveheart who had thought that running towards Sudas with his sword raised would make up for the futility of his own weapons. 'Convince this man of that fact, Anu. And these others as well.'

He saw Atharva had turned his back to the enemy and was about to be attacked from behind by a second opponent. Sudas stepped forward and chopped at the second Anu with a diagonal thrust that severed the man's sword hand, clavicle and half his torso. The man fell, blood and gore bursting forth from his dying frame, nearly splattering his king's boots. 'That is what a man looks like when cut down by an iron sword,' Sudas said as Anu stared down at the butchered corpse of his soldier. 'Try telling him that iron weapons are useless in combat.'

Sudas raised the sword, feeling his arm muscles ache as he did so. The metal was heavy to wield and his arms were not yet used to their weight. 'Or better yet, come try it out for yourself.'

Anu stared at him in a mixture of shock and horror. 'How?' He blurted at last. 'How did you come by such weaponry? I have never heard of it being used by any Trtsu until now!'

Sudas shrugged. 'Why only the Trtsus? It has never

been used by anyone in the known world, to the best of my knowledge. We are the first to wield iron swords. And your gracious soldiers are the first to die beneath them, Anu. As for the swords themselves, they were given to us by our patron deva, Indra himself.'

Anu blanched at that. The soldiers around him gaped and began to mutter among themselves, instantly superstitious. The idea of weapons belonging to the devas was a powerful one and a part of Bharata mythology. Indeed, many believed that iron weapons were the weapons of the gods, the fabled dev astras of yore, and were convinced that mortals were forbidden from using them.

Atharva stepped forward and raised his sword. The weapon and he were bathed in the gore of a dozen enemy bodies, and in his fevered state he looked like an asura out of an ancient mythic tale rather than a civilised Trtsu Bharata kshatriya. *Indra himself fights with the Trtsu today. Come and taste the edge of his iron sword, Anu! Come!'*

12

THE BODIES around Sudas were four deep in places. The reinforcements arriving in their stead had to pick their way past the corpses of their comrades to get to the three Trtsus. There were no more comments or words spoken by the Anu. Yet they came on grimly, wave after wave, dying under the relentless iron blades of Sudas, Bolan and Atharva.

King Anu himself had withdrawn, but he was still standing on the path, watching. Sudas could see his eyes fixed upon himself, watching as Sudas slaughtered man after man who came at him.

Atharva was at the point of collapse. The young Trtsu was barely able to keep his heavy sword up. Holding it in two hands, he swung his whole torso from side to side as he hacked at the oncoming enemy. He had sustained several wounds too, mainly due to his failing strength and bravado. Sudas had told him quietly that he could withdraw, but Atharva had only shaken his head vigorously, without looking at Sudas, and continued fighting.

At a break in the fighting, Sudas glanced up at the patch of sky visible above the rock overhang. It was still bright and he could even see patches of blue sky visible between the brooding clouds. There was sunlight on the upper parts of Uttunga. He prayed that Guru Vashishta had been right about the storm. That was crucial to their strategy. Without the storm, all the iron swords in the world could not save them.

His arms ached to the point where he could feel every tendon of every muscle, and could pinpoint where it attached to the bone. His nerves and muscles stood out in clear relief upon his arms and hands when he looked down at them, visible even through the film of blood and guts and brain matter that stained him. *The offal of battle,* Pijavana had called it.

He knew he should yield his place to the next Trtsu, someone fresher and younger.

But he also knew that his presence, as the king of the Trtsus, wielding the iron sword of Indra, was already becoming an instant legend. He could see the way each successive round of Anu looked at him as they approached. Fearful and awestruck. As if facing a deva descended in an amsa or avatar. Or worse, an asura risen from myth. In a sense, they were both one and the same, for the suras and asuras had been the same tribe before their fall out. The suras came to be called the devas or gods. While the asuras – literally the opponents of the suras – came to be perceived as demoniac monsters. It was not unlike the Dasarajna conflict today.

What did that make him, Sudas and his Trtsus? Devas or asuras? Was there even a difference in war? Once bathed in the offal of battle, were not all men monsters? Was it not Pijavana who had always said after returning home from a battle that he was now ready to return to the life of a man again?

Atharva screamed.

Sudas was busy battling two Anu at once – one of several tactics Anu was attempting in a desperate bid to break through. He could not turn to see what was happening, but from the sounds behind him, he knew that Atharva had been grievously wounded.

'Ucchas!' Sudas shouted as one Anu soldier tried to force him to swing to his extreme left to leave an opening for his fellow on Sudas's extreme right. He hacked right instead of left, killing the other unfortunate, then stepped back and waited for the remaining man to come at him.

'Here, Rajan.' Ucchasrava's voice came from close behind him, underpointed by a grunt as the lieutenant wielded his own heavy weapon against an enemy.

Sudas killed the second soldier and glanced to the side to see Ucchas in Atharva's place. He sensed movement behind and glanced back to see Alena and Daha carrying Atharva's body into the canyon. 'Dead?' He asked curtly.

'Aye,' Ucchas replied as he faced a fresh onslaught. 'You should rest, sire. You have been fighting for half-an-hour without respite.'

Was that all? It felt like the entire day!

'I am waiting...' Sudas began, then broke off. A chorus of yells erupted from outside. He turned to see Anu ducking back, racing back up the path. The soldiers waiting their turn to be slain by the sword of Indra hovered uncertainly, looking back one way then the other, unsure which way to direct their attention.

'...for that,' Sudas finished. He jerked his head at the canyon behind. 'Let's go. Full mounted charge.

Iron swords all. No quarter, no mercy. Tell everyone to strike sideways, aim for the enemy's swords and hack on through to the body. Downwards makes it too difficult to retrieve the iron.'

'Heavy as hell,' Ucchas grumbled. It was the first time Sudas had heard the young lieutenant complain about anything in his life.

Sudas clapped his weary hand on the man's shoulder. 'Get used to it. Someday, all wars will be fought with iron.'

They rode out moments later, wary of an Anu trick. But Sudas knew that the look he had seen in Anu's eyes was not a look of deception – he had reacted spontaneously, running back to investigate the commotion in his own ranks.

And here was the cause.

The Anu were being attacked on their flank.

Almost fifteen score horse riders were fighting fiercely with the Anu. Outnumbered though they were, they had had the element of surprise in their favour – and iron weapons.

Sudas smiled grimly as he saw Ambarish and his other men wielding rough-moulded weapons identical to the ones he held in his hand. His smile turned grimmer as he saw how easily those weapons sliced through the tin armour and copper swords of the Anu. Blood spurted in the slanting sunlight, blood spray and globules catching the rays of sunlight and glittering bright as rubies. Armour cracked, swords split and skulls shattered beneath the iron weapons.

Even the horses of the Anu were unnerved, shrieking and kicking in panic as they sensed the fear of their riders.

Anu's voice roared in the thick of the fight, commanding his men to hold the attack. He was the only thing keeping them still in the fray, Sudas knew. For the superstitious awe that Sudas had seen on Anu's men as they came to die under his blade was now on every single Anu yoddha around. It was an expression of abject terror. What else could be expected from men who believed that the patron deity of their own nation had blessed their opponents with his divine weapons?

Sudas raised his sword, calling out to his men. 'No quarter, no retreat!' he yelled, his voice as fierce as Anu's.

He saw Anu turn to look in his direction as he pressed his legs together to make Saryu dart forward. His brother-in-law's eyes were wide and staring, the pupils tiny dots in beds of white.

He is mortally scared now. He cannot understand how this has come to pass.

Sudas bore down on the rear of the Anu regiment, crying out the Bharata national cry as he came, partly to alert the enemy so that they would turn to face his men. He had no desire to cut down men from behind, since the Anu had all turned to face the other way, shocked by the fresh attack on their flank.

They presumed that all the Trtsus were with me. They never expected us to split up, being so few to begin with. And they cannot fathom where or when we did so.

He smiled to himself again. Splitting his meagre force had been a gamble that seemed insane at first. But Guru Vashishta was wiser and far more learned in the strategies of war than he himself would ever be. Now, that same mad gamble appeared to be an inspired stroke of military genius.

Sudas saw Parni, Kuruk, Ravi, Veda and Assyr fighting fiercely. They looked tired but eager for battle. As did the three thousand warriors who were with them. It was about time too. He had begun to think that Guru Vashishta would keep them occupied until the battle itself was ended. Then again, how could the battle end so long as there were Trtsus left to fight? Guru Vashishta always knew what he was doing. Sudas had never had reason to doubt him, nor had he ever let his guru down. That was the covenant between them.

Three hundred on one front, two hundred on the other, still close to nine hundred Anu between them. Unequal odds.

But the iron made them equals. And then some.

'Bharat-vamsha!' Sudas cried as he tore into the heart of the Anu ranks, swinging his iron sword, reaping blood and gore with ease.

13

THE ANU broke ranks and ran.

It was not a concerted retreat, for Anu himself was still screaming for his men to 'Hold! Hold!'

But how long could men hold against weapons that cut through their armour and snapped their own swords like they were wooden sticks?

The exodus began with a group of soldiers who on seeing Sudas coming at them – swinging his blood-bathed, gore-stained sword – lost their nerve. They turned and rode away, in the direction of the Parusni, towards the main body of their army. The others needed no furhter urging, they simply spurred their own mounts and followed their fleeing comrades.

In moments, the entire Anu regiment was breaking into fragments, most racing away from the fray, fleeing those terrible dev astras and the Sword of Indra. For decades to come, centuries even, the tale of how Indra himself lent his personal weapon to Sudas, king of the Trtsus, would be handed down from grandfather to grandchild. Even the epic events that followed on that historic day could not overshadow the impact that the iron sword made on the Anu psyche.

Anu himself bellowed furiously at the fleeing men.

Then he realised that he stood at risk of being surrounded and captured, or worse. And tried to lead a more dignified official retreat.

'Anu! With me,' he cried, raising his sword and motioning to the krtadhvaj bearer to follow. The bannerman stood out from the ranks of milling horsemen of both sides, and it was that flowing banner that Sudas spotted, attempting to leave the site of the skirmish.

Sudas shouted to Ambarish. 'Stop him!' He pointed with his sword to indicate the banner. Ambarish raised his own bloody sword to show he understood and galloped after Anu, shouting to the Trtsus still between the fleeing enemy and the river. From this side, Salva and Drahkyu understood Sudas's message and led a force to cut the fleeing Anu off on the right.

By the time Sudas caught up with him, Anu was surrounded by a tight web of Trtsus, along with perhaps five score of his closest men. The rest were trickling towards the Parusni in groups of less than a score apiece, not a single one bothering to look behind to see if their king followed.

'Anu,' Sudas said, as Saryu whinnied and pushed her way towards the place where Ambarish and Ucchasrava had pinned Anu.

Anu's horse reared as Saryu approached, baring his teeth as he smelled a mare. A fine bhoja stallion with a warlike temperament, Anu trained the horse to ride down pedestrians who came in his path when riding through cities. Sudas had listened to countless complaints of Anu riding down men, women, children, elders, even brahmins on occasion, simply because they happened to be in his way when he was riding through the streets.

Sudas held Saryu back out of concern for her own safety. She was a fighter but he had no desire to give Anu's stallion a chance to bite a piece out of her rump and then kick her head in. He would like to take everyone under his charge back home alive tonight if possible, even his horse and his dogs.

'You traitor!' Anu cried. His face was red with impotent anger.

'Traitor?' Sudas replied, chuckling. 'That's a term better applied to you, Anu. You betrayed the Bharata nation by allying against its enemies. How could you take military aid from *them*?' He jerked his head in the direction of the river. 'I could understand you aligning with the Purus, the Bhrigus even, despite all our differences. But the Dasyus? The Matsya? The Parsu and the Panis? They are Mleccha in the worst sense of the term, Anu. They desire only to rape this great land and profit from the rewards.'

Anu wiped his mouth with the back of his hand, smearing a spot of blood instead of cleaning it off. 'We all seek to profit from the land, even you, Sudas. Don't be so high and mighty.'

'No, brother Bharata. I wish to build. To grow. To develop. And you could help me do it even now. If you will set down your arms and give up this foolish fight! I am still willing to forgive you your lapses and reunite the Bharata tribes. The foreigners may be our allies, even our trading partners, and may profit under certain conditions and terms. If it is wealth you desire you shall have it in time. But not at this cost! Bharata fighting Bharata? What madness. What a waste.'

Anu pointed at Sudas accusingly. 'You dare offer me terms of surrender? Who do you think you are, Sudas? Son of Indra himself? Have you not seen the sheer numbers of my army? The fortifications I have built upriver and in neighbouring territories? The feats of military engineering my army is capable of? We stopped the Parusni. We can control the rivers! Do you hear me, Sudas? We control the rivers!'

Sudas shook his head in pity. 'There is no need to control the rivers. This land of Five Rivers is bountiful enough.'

Anu stared at Sudas wildly.

'That is why you have barely a tribe's worth of warriors and I have ten times that at my disposal – and much else besides!' Anu said. 'Because you have no ambition, Sudas! Do you not see? He who controls the rivers, controls the earth itself. We do not need gods anymore. We *are* gods now.'

Sudas slid the iron sword from his belt, raising it hilt first to show Anu. 'Yet we still bleed and die as mortals. Do not mistake hubris for ambition, Anu. There is still time. Forsake this mad conflict against your own kind. End this battle and clasp hands with me in brotherhood. I shall not pursue vengeance against you or your own. There shall be no retribution or penalty. Just hand over your weapon to me and withdraw your army. Do it now, before the sun sets, and we shall go back to my hall and drink soma together until the sun rises on a new dawn. What do you say?'

Anu laughed at Sudas. 'You are a fool, Sudas. A hopeless people-loving fool. Do you not understand yet? There is only one person that matters in this world, yourself. All that you do for others, it shall count for naught in the end. A man may only work and reap rewards for his own satisfaction. That is the law of the world.'

Sudas stared at the hilt of the iron sword before slipping it back into his belt. 'Then you will not surrender?'

Anu laughed again in response. 'Mad man. You are the one who should be begging to surrender. Although I will not accept your surrender now. For you have shed too much Anu blood. That is unforgivable.'

'It was done in self-defence,' Sudas said sorrowfully. 'Not once have we attacked you, we only raised our swords when you came at us.'

Anu waved his hand dismissively. 'You are guilty

and condemned by me. Every last one of you will die here before the dawn breaks on the new day tomorrow. We shall hunt you down and slay you no matter if it takes every resource at our command. You cannot hope to survive.'

Sudas shrugged. 'We survived this long. Even though you threw your best and bravest at us.'

Anu clenched his fists until the knuckles whitened. 'I have more men. Braver. Better. And many more things besides. Now let me and my yoddhas pass or kill us if you dare. I am done bandying words with you, Trtsu!'

Sudas nodded to his lieutenants. They moved their horses to let Anu and his men ride away.

'Why did you let them go, Rajan?' Ambarish asked fiercely, 'We could have ended this here and now! All we had to do was kill Anu.'

Sudas looked at Ambarish sympathetically. 'And act against our own dharma? Nay. All that would have happened was that the other nine kings would have apportioned his assets amongst themselves and continued against us. So long as Anu leads the enemy, I know his tactics and his strategy. My own response is based on that knowledge.'

He gestured towards the river. 'Besides, the enemy

is already committed. Anu's surrender or death would not cause them to withdraw. They mean to have Trtsu territory with Anu's aid or without it.'

Ambarish subsided, seeing the sense in Sudas's words.

Sudas raised his voice to make sure he was heard by all his lieutenants and the rest as well. It was still a small enough band. 'We fight on to the end, brothers. If they will not end it, then we must.'

14

Sudas reached the base point and turned Saryu around. She snorted the dust of the mountain path out of her nostrils and tapped the ground with her forelegs before settling. Ambarish, Ucchas, Bolan and the others turned their mounts as well, looking outward across the kusa sea to the river. The view from here was spectacular, an epic vista encompassing the vast flatland plains of the Five Rivers all the way up to the foothills of the mountain ranges in the north. To the south and west too, they could see for yojanas. The setting sun's light cast great shadows across the landscape, turning it into a child's playground with clay soldiers and figurines set out in mock battle.

The battlefield lay below them, more clearly visible from up here than below. It was to see this that Sudas had brought his lieutenants up here for a rendezvous.

'The Anu have retreated back across the river,' Daha said, pointing at the tin-armoured horsemen bunched together in a ragged group on the far bank of the Parusni.

'Licking their wounds and crying for their mothers!' Kuruk said contemptuously.

Even at this distance, Sudas could see that many of the horsemen were discarding their armour and lying on the grass bank, while others stood about talking and gesturing agitatedly. 'They are out of the fray for the time being,' he said.

A cheer went up from his men. He smiled indulgently but added a word of caution: 'But they will be back for vengeance. You know the Anu.'

The cheer died down. It was true. The Anu never let an insult or a perceived insult pass by unrequited. Today's double blows were a huge attack on their honour and pride. They would not miss a chance to stick the blade into Trtsu flesh.

'Look, Rajan. They have brought the elephants across.' Veda pointed. The young man was barely a few years older than Indrani, his almost hairless face testifying his youth. But he was a shrewd observer and a quick study. Hair could grow later, bodies built up, skills acquired, but the basic talents of a warrior were either present in childhood or could never be learned, Sudas believed. Veda was a young general in the making. The youth frowned now, 'What are they trying to do? Why bring them across the kusa?'

Sudas looked in the direction Veda was pointing. Scattered amongst the waving kusa fields were grey hulks, thudding sombrely along, their trunks wavering to and fro, tails flicking. They were clearly in some kind of organised formation, one elephant every ten yards or so. 'They are ensuring that we do not conceal more archers in the grass. I think they shall keep the elephants beating the grass until we are routed now.'

'So, then we cannot resort to the same tactic you used before, Rajan?' Assyr asked, sounding disappointed. The bright-blue-eyed man had come as a foreigner to their town as part of a trading party, when he was but an infant. The murder of his mother and father in a trading dispute by Bharatas – by Anu tradesmen, in point of fact – had led Sudas to proclaim that the infant would be granted shelter and care among the Trtsus for as long as he desired. Three decades later, Assyr still stayed on and proudly counted himself a Trtsu.

'You shall have your chance some other day, Assyr,' Sudas said. 'So long as there are men such as Anu, there will always be wars and tactics to deploy.'

Assyr nodded, his blue eyes flashing.

Across the river, the troop movement had increased in speed and intensity. Sudas watched as troops poured across the bridge in an endless succession – horsemen of different nations, footsoldiers and even the dreaded chariots.

'Wheelchairs,' Parni said mockingly. 'For old men too feeble to ride or run.'

'Do not underestimate those wheeled chairs,' Ravi said quietly. The grey-bearded man was among Sudas's oldest lieutenant, and as evidence of his long experience and age, he had only a left hand and the stump of a right hand, but his presence of mind in the heat of battle made him worth a score of four-handed men. 'Deployed correctly on the right terrain, chariots can devastate entire regiments on their own. They can turn and wheel ten directions at once, until you wonder if there was one chariot or ten of them against you.'

Salva nodded. 'It is true. I have seen Assyr's people rout my Parsu brethren in the Behistani hills, using just a half score of chariots with two men apiece against an entire regiment of Parsu footsoldiers.'

'Yes, but we are mounted,' Alena argued, 'And we have iron swords now!'

Sudas spoke up, 'Even iron swords are of no use when you are being fired on by an archer on a chariot from a distance. That is why the wheelchairs have two men, one to pilot the horses and the other to aim the arrows. And those archers are experts at shooting at great speeds, while to shoot them is nigh impossible even if one is standing still.'

They watched silently as an entire score of chariots rolled across the wooden bridge and onto the dusty flat ground beyond the kusa grass – the same open field Anu and his surviving yoddhas had crossed when they retreated earlier.

Thsang's voice called out from behind. 'Rajan! Gurudev approaches!'

Sudas turned to see Thsang point upwards. The Himavat native would be the only one to be looking up the mountain when everyone else was looking downwards. Only a mountain man would be wary of attacks from above. In this case, there was no imminent danger, just the flowing red ochre robes of the guru and his long lustrous white beard, both flapping in the wind, which had increased steadily over the past hour or two.

Sudas dismounted and went forward as the guru descended the last few yards to approach the relatively flat resting spot chosen as base point.

'Pranaam, Gurudev,' he said, touching the guru's feet reverentially.

'Ayushmaanbhava, Rajan Sudas,' Vashishta said. 'You have done well thus far in the battle of the Dasarajna.'

'All credit to your teachings and to the wisdom you imparted to your humble shishya, Mahadev,' Sudas said with genuine humility.

'Even so, you made excellent use of very limited resources and the geographical theatre of war.'

Sudas inclined his head again, keeping his palms joined together in the namasakara gesture. 'The iron weapons were a gift from Indra himself,' he said.

Vashishta chuckled, straightening his beard which was being whipped to and fro by the errant wind. 'You might say that. Aided of course by a very good blacksmith I guided,' he leaned closer, intending the next words to be heard only by Sudas, 'and a secret element that makes the iron workable even with alloy tools.'

Sudas nodded, knowing better than to ask any questions here and now. The guru had promised divine weapons and he had delivered them in ample quantity; that was all that mattered. When it was appropriate for him to know more about the working and manipulation of iron in the forge, the guru would induct him into those mysteries as well. He had the warrior's infinite patience in such matters and was content in knowing what he needed to know and doing his given task for the moment.

'Now, Sudas,' Guru Vashishta said, 'it is the next and final phase of the battle that will determine whether your dream of a united Bharata nation will live forever or die today on this field with you and your loved ones. Are you ready to undertake that last trial?'

'Aye, Gurudev,' Sudas said.

Guru Vashishta nodded. 'Then you must do exactly as I advise, no matter how reckless it seems or how heavy the cost to your numbers. Do you follow my meaning, Sudas?'

Sudas's heart skipped a beat. He swallowed dryly. 'Must it involve heavy losses to my men?' He nodded towards the group of lieutenants waiting for him to finish the private conversation with the preceptor; the rest of their band was at the foot of the mountain, by the thicket, awaiting their return. 'We are so few now and have been decimated already. I cannot bear to ask many more to lay down their lives for what may be a hopeless cause.' The face of young Atharva, fevered and half-mad with sickness, flashed before his eyes.

Guru Vashishta's entire aspect and tone changed at once. 'If it is hopeless then give it up at once. Why do you throw away your life and theirs on a worthless cause?'

Sudas bowed his head. 'Forgive me, Gurudev, I meant only that it seems worthless in the face of human life and loss. You know that I have devoted my life to furthering my father's and his father's dreams of building a united Bharata nation. I am willing to die here on this field today for that cause. But I am loathe to ask more good men to lay down their lives as well.'

'Then send them away, ask them to surrender their arms to Anu and throw themselves at his mercy. Will he spare them now? Will he forgive them, embrace and kiss them and treat them like his sons and family?'

Sudas shook his head. 'He will torture and execute them as examples. They have been a thorn in his side, as have I. They are the symbols of all the rails against the very cause of this war.'

Guru Vashishta bared his teeth. 'So then they make up the Bharata nation you speak of building, do they not? These are the first bricks you have fired, bricks which shall be laid down as your foundation, are they not?'

'In a manner of speaking, yes, they are,' Sudas said.

The guru smiled unexpectedly. 'Then you do them a great service, Sudas. You are making them founding fathers of this proud nation you dream of building! All who die today on this field are martyrs to the cause of the Bharat-vamsha. Would you deprive them of that supreme honour? Take away their assured place in the itihasa of this new nation?'

Sudas shook his head. 'Nay.' His voice was suddenly thick with emotion.

Vashishta clapped a great hand on Sudas's shoulder. 'Good. Then stop fretting about your men. Their death and your own is assured today, Sudas. All you can do now is make it count for something. Give the world an example that will shine like a beacon for ages to come. Let the world never forget this day when Ten Kings warred against One.'

15

BY THE time Sudas and his lieutenants had descended from base point to the thicket, the sun was on the horizon. Some of the men mentioned it aloud, glancing at their king. Under kshatriya dharma, it was obligatory on both sides to cease fighting at sundown. Even individual fighters were expected to stop fighting and back away. Sudas's grandfather Divodasa had even followed the ancient practice of inviting his opponents to drink and dine with him around his campfire after the day's fighting was done.

Sudas gestured with a tilt of his head in the direction of the river, even though the thicket concealed the field of battle from view at present. 'Do you think they appeared to be withdrawing from the field?' he asked his lieutenants.

They shook their heads.

Ucchasrava shook his fist at the western sky. 'We cut them to shreds by day; we will cut them by night as well.'

'Aye!' chorused the rest.

Just then a furry shape came bounding over the last rise, woofing happily. It was followed by several more, all woofing and barking joyfully. The horses neighed irritably but did not shy away, they were familiar with the scent of these hounds.

'Sarama!' Sudas cried. The familiar furry face looked up at him and woofed happily, dancing circles around Saryu. As if in response, the mare raised her head proudly and sidestepped clip-clop, clip-clop in a little dance of her own. Sudas laughed. 'Enough, you two! We still have a battle to fight.'

At the thicket, young Bhargu was waiting with several more hounds. They all leaped forward, barking joyfully at the sight of their master and king. Thanks to Sarama's leadership, they knew that Sudas, her master, was their master as well. There was also the fact that Sudas treated them and fed them better than anyone else.

Sudas dismounted and spent a moment being licked and pawed and fawned over by more canine snouts, jaws, tongues, and paws than he could count at a glance. 'I take this to mean you completed your last chore, boy,' he shouted to Bhargu over the uproar.

'Aye, sire,' the boy responded. 'You can see the smoke all the way out here. It is a great blaze.'

He pointed northeastwards. Sudas stood and looked. The others turned to look as well, curious.

Far in the distance, at what appeared to be the horizon line – although he knew it was only a few yojanas away – curls of smoke were rising in the air, caught by the slanting light of the setting sun.

'Rajan, what is burning?' asked Veda.

'Our home,' Sudas answered grimly.

Exclamations rose from the men. 'You torched the town, Rajan?'

'Aye,' Sudas said. 'I left word with young Bhargu here that if we did not return before sundown, he was to fire the houses. The fire would have spread quickly enough on its own, I warrant.'

'Like a forest blaze,' Bhargu said. 'It was all I could do to get the dogs out in time. They followed me here. There was nothing I could do to stop them, sire.'

'That is as well,' Sudas said. 'Homes can be rebuilt.

But these hounds are no less my family and my warriors than any of you!'

'Rajan, what purpose does burning the city serve?' Kuruk asked curiously.

Drahkyu answered for Sudas. 'It sends a message to the enemy that we are prepared to fight to the last man. That we shall give no quarter and expect none in return.' He glanced at his king to be assured that he had spoken correctly. Sudas nodded.

'It is the ultimate sacrifice of a warrior,' said Daha. 'To set fire to one's own home means that he has already deprived the enemy of any loot or plunder, leaving only honour as the goal for the battle.' He glanced at Sudas. 'Among my people, at such times even our womenfolk shut themselves into the houses with our young'uns and elders, before we light the fires. To deprive the enemy of the satisfaction of ravishing or torturing them under capture.'

Sudas's cheek twitched involuntarily. 'I have heard of that custom. Among Bharatas, we do not consider our family our property; hence the practice has no relevance.'

He did not look down towards the thicket. Sudevi, Indrani and Indraut were there, he knew. He would have dearly wished them to be upon the summit of Uttunga, with Guru Vashishta. But the preceptor had been adamant that only he could stay alone on the peak, performing the final yagna. Sudas considered sending them to the box canyon to hide, with a few warriors to protect them in case they were chanced upon. But with that side already overrun by enemy troops, he knew that they would almost certainly be spotted going into the canyon, making them an easy target.

For better or worse, they would have to ride with him now, come hell or high water.

He gave his band their final instructions. Most of these were directed at the lieutenants who would then command their individual units. This delegation of command made for more effective communication and also fostered a sense of pride among the individual units and men, for they felt they were each performing a specific given task with measurable results. It was far more motivational than the all for one and one for all approach that the Anu followed. Sudas swore by it. However, this also meant that if an individual unit or two failed their given task, the entire strategy might go awry. But he had faith enough in his men that they would never let him down, whatever the odds. And that in turn bred fierce devotion and loyalty in the men, driving them to do whatever it took to succeed at their individual chores, no matter the risk or the cost.

For once, his heart was heavier than usual when giving the final commands. In every battle, he sent men out to risk their lives. Many would come back maimed, grievously injured, or not at all.

But this was the first battle from which none would have anything to return to. Their homes were burned, the land overrun by the enemy, their authority disputed, their ideals scorned, their king opposed by his rivals. What motivation could they have to succeed at their tasks? Even if they performed like champions, like maha yoddhas, what reward could he promise them for their achievements? He had nothing to give, not even a homeland, let alone a home.

He finished, wished them all well quietly, and then led them in a moment of silent prayer. Everyone knew that Guru Vashishta was staging a yagna atop the peak of Mount Uttunga even now, to appease their patron deities and pray for their success in this final battle of the day. *And the final battle of their lives*, Sudas thought. For he knew he would not see any of their faces again.

They finished and he nodded, tacitly giving permission to break away and proceed.

As he was turning Saryu's head, they called out to him.

'Rajan.'

He turned back.

As one, the entire company, men, women, and young boys, performed the horse salute.

It was a difficult maneuver. Forcing untrained horses to do it could result in severe injury, even broken legs and the loss of the horse itself. But Trtsu Bharatas were bonded to their horses from the time they could walk, and their mounts were attuned to their wishes. Affection could often achieve what even the harshest discipline could not aspire for.

Every horse in the company bent its forelegs, bowing down as its rider raised his or her sword in the final salute, swords pointed outwards, eyes fixed towards the sky.

'*WITH INDRA!*' they roared in a single voice.

'*WITH VARUNA!*' they roared again.

'*WITH MITRA!*' they concluded.

Then they lowered the swords to point below Sudas's feet.

'*WITH SUDAS!*

The horses reared back to all fours, a harder action than the actual bowing. The riders used their legs to turn their mounts, and began riding away without another word. Their swords remained in their hands. There would be no need to sheathe them again now, Sudas knew.

In moments they were all gone, leaving only Sudas, Sudevi, Indrani, Indraut and a small band of warriors he had hand-picked for this last mission. He watched the last horse's tail flick as its rump turned around the edge of the thicket, then was lost from sight.

He looked around at the dogs. Sarama was sitting on her haunches, tongue lolling, waiting. Her brood and extended clan sat or lay around her. They were a motley mix of breeds, colours and ages, some barely pups, others so old and feeble their paws shook as they walked. But they were his as well to command and he would use them as best as he could. That was his prerogative and his dharma – to use every resource at his disposal, so long as it could be used. Regardless of the cost.

Such was the dharma of a king.

16

THE SETTING sun was on his right as he rode down the skirt of Uttunga. To one side lay the kusa fields, dominated by the caparisoned elephants, lowing and stamping their way through the grass. Footsoldiers had joined the ranks of the pachyderms, thrashing and hacking at the tall stalks as they trampled the grass down. Their numbers were heart-stopping.

Never before in his life had Sudas seen such a vast fighting force deployed in a single battlefield. Large forces were known to have been commanded by kings in some earlier conflicts too, particularly in the Arya-Parsu wars and the wars with the Assyr or the Steppe Raiders, but rarely was a force of this size actually thrown into battle, and that too against such a puny opposition. Most regiments remained in van or flank positions, present for the purpose of intimidation and to facilitate negotiation, rather than actual deployment. Not only was the management of such a large army daunting, it was also extremely difficult, if not impossible, to maintain constant communication with so many men. At the same time, the vagaries of any terrain made it preferable to break down each battle into a succession of smaller skirmishes. In fact, it was customary to send forward champions for individual fights instead of pitting thousands of men against one another. While champions on both sides decided the outcome of a war, the rest of the men usually sat and watched the fight as though it were some entertainment – eating, drinking and applauding boisterously. The discipline and intensity of such a massive army could only be maintained for a very short time.

But this was precisely the reason why Guru Vashishta had devised his plan. Everything Sudas had done since afternoon had been designed to provoke the Ten Kings into damming the river and sending the majority of their force across the Parusni.

He had succeeded.

The enemy was in Trtsu land now, and it would take more than tactics or strategy to chase them out. Certainly more than a force of a few thousand.

But he still had to adhere to the plan, until the moment came. And that moment depended on, of all things, the weather.

He glanced up at the sky. While several of the brooding clouds from that afternoon still hovered overhead, the sky was clearly visible in patches, lit by the saffron flames of the sinking sun. It seemed like any other evening during the monsoon. Then he heard the distant growl of thunder in the northwest and remembered that it had been sounding every few minutes for the past few hours. Still, it sounded remote and so removed from where he was that he found it hard to believe that it could truly affect his situation. Yet Guru Vashishta had been unequivocal in his prediction. The storm would burst right here on this plain, at the foot of Uttunga, before the sun had fully set.

Even so, despite his unwavering faith in his guru and in the ability of humankind to acquire and utilise knowledge – Veda, to use the proper word – it was a daunting realisation that his life and the lives of all his people now rested solely on the caprices of the weather.

He glanced back and saw Indrani and Indraut riding close behind him, hugging his flanks as he had ordered, with Sudevi bringing up the rear. Behind her was a semi-circular cluster of Trtsu warriors. Atharva would have been among them had he survived but they had left his body in the canyon, to be sanctified and cremated later – if there was a later. The formation was designed to protect the children and Sudevi but he knew that with the variety of forces pitted against them, no formation would hold for long under a full onslaught. They were safe only till the enemy realised that he and his family were part of this band; after that, they would throw their might against them to ensure their annihilation. The main challenge for them now was to ride as fast as possible to their destination – the far side of the river, into the enemy camp itself.

They came around the end of the tree line and then they were in the open, visible to all on the plain below. Sudas picked up pace, urging Saryu. The dogs were racing alongside with impressive speed, Sarama leading her pack with great bounding strides. They flanked Sudas's party on either side, forming an extra layer of protection. As a mother herself, Sarama understood that her primary mission was to keep the enemy away from Indrani, Indraut and Sudevi. Sudas glanced at her as she came alongside Saryu and she jerked her muzzle at him in the semblance of a bark, unable to make the actual sound. All her energy was devoted to maintaining the gruelling pace and keeping up with one of the fastest horses in Trtsu territory. Saryu did not spare her either, for she too was well aware of what was at stake here.

Sudas rode down the sloping dirt path at attack speed. He was still high enough to be able to view the other units as they fanned out to their respective destinations.

He saw Ucchasrava, Kavi, Kuruk, Thsang and Alena enter the kusa fields from five separate points, racing directly towards the elephants. Each of them was accompanied by a few score of men apiece, spread out to cover maximum ground. The kusa sea parted before their galloping horses like water before a nest of crocodiles racing towards their prey. The elephant mahouts saw them coming and shouted warnings to the footsoldiers. Archers had been mounted on the elephants and they fixed arrows to bows at once and took aim. Sudas saw the first volley go awry because the Trtsus were riding fast and the wind was growing in strength.

On the western horizon, the sun was nearly down.

The sky was still clear in patches, but he could see a great mass of storm clouds drifting in from the northwest. The thunder boomed again and it was much closer this time. Then he caught the flash of lightining from the corner of his right eye, but he did not turn to look.

Far ahead, closer to the river, Ambarish, Daha, Salva, Assyr, and Drahkyu's units were converging on the cavalry that had crossed over and were massed on the Trtsu side of the bank. Theirs was the largest force: almost three thousand warriors. They were charging at the enemy in what probably seemed to be a suicidal run. Three thousand riders against almost ten times that many! Even at a glance, Sudas could tell that there were easily ten thousand armoured cavalrymen massed already, with as many more in the process of crossing. It was that group's job to ensure that more cavalry crossed over and joined in the fight, and to do that they were throwing their lives away in a fierce but hopeless bid.

He saw the enemy horsemen form a line facing the approaching Trtsu, then mill about in some confusion as they realised they were being attacked on not one but five separate fronts. The Trtsu bore down on the enemy from all sides, splitting up their force into smaller units, which in turn split up into bands of a score apiece, with the deliberate intent of confusing the enemy and forcing fights to break out all across the riverbank.

Even at this distance, despite the pounding hooves of his band's horses and the rumbling thunder overhead, Sudas heard the sound of his Trtsus clash with the enemy. He heard the already familiar and satisfying sound of iron blades crack open tin and copper shields and armour, shatter swords and spears. He could also see the unmistakable crimson of blood splatter in great arcs. The Trtsu had crashed into the enemy with such force that at least a score of men had gone down in a seething mass of chaos – horses, men, and weapons all falling together in a deadly tangle. That was common in any massed cavalry attack, but for a force so tiny to attack a greater army with such ferocity was bloodcurdling.

17

H<small>E</small> <small>HEARD</small> the trumpeting of elephants to his right and turned his head, keeping it pressed low against Saryu's mane as she carried him relentlessly forward. Impressively, Sarama was still racing alongside, keeping pace with unwavering stamina.

Over in the kusa fields, Ucchasrava and the other four lieutenants had met the enemy as well. Theirs was not as fierce a clash as the other Trtsus on the riverbank. Indeed, their charge was not directed at the footsoldiers at all, but at the elephants.

Sudas watched as each Trtsu directed his arrows and sword blades, depending on their distance, at the grey lumbering beasts. He heard elephants low in pain as they were struck by arrows or hacked at by swords – iron swords, tough enough to easily cut through elephant hide, causing serious injury and great pain. The footsoldiers were totally unprepared for this method of attack. They tried to engage the Trtsus, but Ambarish and the others were simply hitting and running – they would wound an elephant, then ride past, moving to the next one. In moments, the entire kusa field was a mass of chaos as elephants began trumpeting in agony and running amok in fear and confusion. Many crushed their own soldiers underfoot, and threw their mahouts and archers off in the throes of pain. Sudas saw men fly and fall with sickening force, others were crumpled like mud pots under huge punishing feet. A bucking elephant was a terrible thing. Two score frenzied elephants were a riot out of control.

He saw some of his own Trtsu men get caught in the aftermath of the chaos they had created. A rider who looked very much like Alena was struck by an elephant foot swinging back and fell off his horse onto his head. Sudas did not see him rise again. Another band of Trtsus came under fire from the archers atop three elephants clustered close together; he saw at least a handful of his men go down with spurting wounds. They succeeded in getting close enough to the elephants but the mahouts were prepared by this time and used the beasts to pound the Trtsus down when they got close enough. He saw more of his men fall as enemy footsoldiers surrounded them and pulled them off their horses, stabbing and hacking at them mercilessly, then looked away. With barely a few thousand Trtsus against ten thousand footsoldiers and a hundred elephants, heavy casualties were certain, but it still pained him to see men throw their lives away like that.

However, the tactic was working; the first wounded elephants were turning back, instinctively seeking to return to a more familiar place, which in this case was the far side of the river where they had come from. They were all hurt, some seriously wounded and in terrible pain. Their trumpeting cries were distressing to Sudas as well; he hated harming such beautiful beasts no less than he felt saddened by the loss of his own men, but they were warriors on a battlefield too and as such, subject to the conditions of war.

The wounded elephants began running back towards the riverbank, their individual pain adding to the collective agony, and finally a stampede that was slowly picking speed. Sudas saw that even the unharmed elephants were trumpeting in alarm and turning around, some crushing footsoldiers or unseating archers as they did so, in comradeship with the suffering of their injured fellows. In a moment, it would turn into a complete stampede. One hundred stampeding elephants across a field where footsoldiers were effectively hidden by the tall grass could wreak terrible havoc. Besides, where could the soldiers run for cover? He guessed that a great number of the enemy soldiers would be crushed or maimed by the stampeding beasts before they could get out of the way. Some even began flinging down their weapons and running back in the direction of their camp, adding to the riot.

He would have smiled grimly if not for the fact that his own men were caught in the riot, and were likely to die either under the feet of the stampeding elephants or by the swords of the enemy soldiers. They had succeeded in creating the stampede he had ordered, but it was as suicidal a mission as the other group had undertaken.

On the riverbank, the Trtsus led by Ambarish and the other lieutenants were faring surprisingly better, for now at least.

The ferocity of their first charge, and the splitting up of their force into smaller units had dissolved the enemy ranks into total chaos. Accustomed to and expecting a straightforward full frontal charge, the enemy cavalry did not know how to respond to a hundred individual units rather than a single massed force. Added to that was the iron factor – the ease with which the iron swords were hacking through their armour and weapons had unnerved the enemy, who were witnessing the power of these new metal blades for the first time. If word had spread after the Anu defeat, it would only have added to their sense of fear and awe. The Swords of Indra were an awe-inspiring sight in action, wielded by Trtsus who were fighting like devas protected by a divine kavach or the gift of immortality.

Sudas saw some of his men fall as well, mostly to arrows or thrown spears and javelins. But the discrepancy in the casualty rate was still staggering: The Trtsu bands were cutting down a score of enemy for every Trtsu, and were still going strong, reaping a bloody harvest. It was a massacre, but not the kind that Anu had promised.

He allowed himself to feel no pleasure, for he knew that eventually the superior forces would win over the situation. However fiercely the Trtsus fought, however effective their iron swords were against the enemy, they were like a single goat nipping at a pride of lions. The goat might nip a lion or two and draw blood, but it would be killed and devoured by the lions sooner rather than later. Thirty thousand horsemen against three thousand. What else could one expect?

Still, for the moment, they had accomplished their mission, which was to create enough chaos by the riverbank to draw more troops across to the Trtsu side, and to keep them engaged long enough for Sudas and his band to ride across the bridge.

But there was a third front and it came into view now, as he passed the extremities of Uttunga's outskirts and in clear sight of the river straight ahead. To his left lay the long straight dirt field which led to the box canyon and around Uttunga's flank. On that front lay the most deadly enemy weapons of all, their chariots!

Already, the footsoldiers massed on Sudas's left hand were shouting and pointing towards him and his galloping band. Despite the chaos on the riverbank and in the kusa fields, he had been spotted. Beyond the footsoldiers, who were not much of a threat since they could hardly catch him and his people on foot, lay the score of wheeled death machines that struck such fear into the hearts of Bharata kshatriyas everywhere.

He glimpsed several of the charioteers turning their

horses towards the riverbank. They would aim to cut off Sudas and his band before they reached the bridge. What was more, coming at Sudas's band from the left flank, they would be able to attack with arrows and spears with impunity, while Sudas and his team could hardly fight back effectively. Not when their main goal was to cross the bridge. Besides, if they had to slow down or stop and engage the chariot, they were done for anyway. It was physically impossible for a few score riders to hold their own against a thousand chariots!

But that was why he had delegated the remainder of his force to Bolan, Ravi, Veda, Parni and Daha, all of whom had some experience battling chariots. And just as he feared they would be too late, he heard the whoops and ululating cat-calls from the far left as the last band of Trtsus came around the skirt of Uttunga and rode hard towards the chariots of the enemy.

The chariots closest to the mountain had already turned back towards the river. They were caught unawares by the charging Trtsus who appeared suddenly in their rear.

Sudas glimpsed arrows flying, striking the charioteers and their archers. Two, three, five, a half score chariots were rendered useless by the expertly aimed arrows of Bolan and his team. The barrage continued even as the Trtsu band raced towards the main force of the chariot company, forcing them to choose between facing this dangerous new enemy and defending themselves or chasing after the other band of Trtsus who were in any case heading into Ten Kings' territory like lambs into the mouths of lions.

The chariots turned back to deal with Bolan and his men. The mission had succeeded.

Sudas felt a surge of satisfaction and with it came the pang of despair. All of his lieutenants and their teams had done their given tasks. If only they and he could live so he could reward them for their achievements.

Far to his right flank, the last rays of the setting sun faded away as twilight fell over the Parusni plain.

And then with a loud crash, thunder exploded overhead.

18

A SUDDEN DARKNESS fell over the world. It was so abrupt, Sudas thought a veil had been drawn across his eyes. He reached up and rubbed his face and eyes, only to realise that there was nothing there. He glanced around and saw the shapes of his children and wife and the others limned in a strange purplish hue. It was not unusual to see the world bathed in purplish light at twilight, but the darkness coupled with the coloured light was what surprised him. Saryu instinctively slowed her frenetic pace, and to his right, Sudas heard Sarama's familiar inquisitive bark, even though the animals could see far better than him and his companions.

He looked up at the sky and was startled to see a cloudbank even denser and darker than the one that had hung over the plain that morning. Where had it come from all of a sudden? And then he realised that while he had been preoccupied with watching the skirmishes on the ground, the clouds had been gathering overhead for hours. And now that the sun was down, the storm had come, exactly as Guru Vashishta had predicted.

He slowed down, aware from the cessation of sounds that the fighting across the plain had briefly ceased. The elephants were still stampeding and their screams and cries, coupled with the panicked screams of dying horses and men, continued unabated. If anything, the sudden change in weather had only caused the stampeding elephants to lose further control as they rampaged about in a mad fury.

Sudas heard shouts in the enemy ranks, a hundred yards to his left and two hundred yards to the right. All around him a clamour arose and even in the dim purplish light, he saw hands raised, pointing heavenwards. Even before he followed their gaze, he knew where they were pointing and at what.

Bringing Saryu to a complete halt, he turned in his saddle and looked up at the summit of Mount Uttunga. He had to crane his neck up as high as it could go to see the top of the mountain from here. He guessed that for some reason a few of the men must have kept an eye on the mountain peak even before the darkness fell. *Or perhaps they were looking up at the sky and saw the light shining on the peak.* Either way, the entire army of the Ten Kings seemed to have been alerted and aware of what was happening.

The summit seemed to be ablaze. That was his first impression.

Beside him, Indrani's voice came in hushed awe, 'Look! The mountain is on fire!'

That was how it seemed. All he could see from here was a great fire raging at the very top of Uttunga. What did that mean? Was that the yagna fire the guru had spoken of? But Sudas had never seen a yagna fire so large, nor could he fathom how the guru could have generated such a huge fire on Agni's Cradle.

Then he remembered the chores that Ambarish and other Trtsus had been doing for the guru for half the day. He was only aware of some part of what was to come now, not every detail of how it was being accomplished. Somehow, the guru must have had his men bring up material that could create such a great flame at the summit and he had lit it now to attract the eyes of the enemy.

Remember, Sudas. While all eyes are on Uttunga's

peak, you must ride with your family to safety. Do not stop until you have crossed the rocky road!

All eyes were now on Uttunga's peak. But Sudas found himself unable to move. That solitary flame blazing at the top of the mountain was a powerful sight to behold in this unexpectedly darkened purple world. It was hard to believe that no supernatural power was at work.

'Look!' Indraut's voice said, excited. 'It's Guru Vashishta!'

And it was.

Sudas could see the shape of the guru's form, clad in his ochre robes, white beard lit by the glow of the flames behind him, staff in hand. Somehow the fire seemed to be below and in front of the guru as well as behind, lighting him from his feet upwards to produce a peculiar, unnerving effect.

Across the plain, the enemy reacted with audible awe. They were all superstitious people, whatever their tribe or nation, and Guru Vashishta's reputation was beyond that of any ordinary brahmin. There were many who believed that he was thousands of years old and had walked the earth at the very beginning of time, with the other saptarishis, the sacred seven sages who pre-dated humankind. Sudas, however, thought it more likely that Vashishta was the youngest in a long line of Vashishtas, all of whom had an inevitable family resemblance and passed on the same lore and knowledge – the sacred Vedas. This was the reason they appeared to be the same person, present generation after generation.

But now, even he wondered.

Lightning flashed overhead, followed instantly by a crack of thunder so overwhelming that Sudas ducked his head instinctively. He raised it slowly, feeling foolish, but that boom had been so close it felt as if it had exploded over his own head! And then came the lightning, brilliant and crackling with power, like Indra's own vajra.

'Look!' Sudevi shouted this time, and Sudas dared to raise his head again to gaze up at the summit.

Guru Vashishta had raised both his hands and was appealing to Indra.

Even though he could not hear the guru's actual words from this great distance, Sudas knew that was what the guru was doing.

Indra was the patron deity of the Bharata Trtsus. And Guru Vashishta, as their preceptor and chief purohit, was staging a yagna in Indra's honour, appealing to the god of storms to aid his human followers in their hour of need. That gesture, of raising his hands to the sky, was a normal part of the yagna. Sudas could almost hear the shlokas the guru would be chanting at this moment, for he had heard them countless times since birth. If not the precise shloka that was on the guru's lips at this very moment, then one quite similar to it in essence and meaning:

वि स्द्यो विश्वा दृंहितान्य् एषाम् इन्द्रः पुरः सहसा सप्त ददिः ।
व्य् आनर्वस्य् तृत्सवे गयम् भाग् जेष्म पूरुं विदथे मृध्रवाचम् ॥ ७ ०१८ १३
नि गव्यवो ऽनवो द्रुह्यवश् च षष्टिः शता सुषुपुः षट् सहस्रा ।
षष्टिर् वीरासो अधि षड् दुवोयु विश्वेद् इन्द्रस्य वीर्या कृतानि ॥ ७ ०१८ १४

Another great clap of thunder exploded, seeming to come almost at the exact same moment as the flash of lightning. Sudas knew that the gap between the time when the lightning flashed and the thunder boomed indicated how far away the lightning had struck. For every one score counts, it would be a score of yojana distant.

Simultaneous lightning and thunder meant only one thing – the lightning was striking the place where you stood!

In this case, close enough.

The bolt of lightning struck the peak of Uttunga.

Sudas heard a chorus of gasps and shouts. Across the plain, everyone had eyes only for the peak of Uttunga and the phenomenon unfolding atop the mountain.

The lightning bolt struck the peak and a storm of sparks exploded behind Guru Vashishta.

Cries erupted across the plain, punctuated by other human sounds of awe and fear. Thunder drowned them all out.

Another bolt of lightning struck the peak. It lit Guru Vashishta with such blinding light that Sudas felt as if the guru's silhouette had been seared into his mind's eye forever. He shut his eyes and could still see the guru's shape, standing with arms outstretched, appealing to Indra.

Indra boomed in the form of thunder again, answering his loyal priest's call.

Again, lightning struck. And yet again. Accompanied by ominous claps of thunder.

So close were the lightning cracks and thunderbolts that each loud clap seemed to roll into the next, almost as if the gods were having heated debates with one another.

It was hard to not hear that sound and believe that it was a divine voice. Indra venting his rage on those who had dared to attack his people.

Sudas did not look up this time. He kept his eyes averted from the peak, realising that to continue staring up was to risk blindness, either temporary or permanent.

He looked around. Sudevi and the children had covered their eyes as well.

The dogs were mewling. They did not like whatever was happening. Sarama yelped at the thunder then subsided, intimidated by its sheer force and intensity.

Another jagged sword of lightning snaked down and struck the peak of Uttunga. Even without looking up, Sudas could see it had been hit. The bolt hit the mountain with a force so tremendous, he could feel it all the way down here. Saryu shook on her feet as if jostled by an earthquake. She whinnied in alarm, her emotions echoed by all the other horses across the plain.

Something resonated within the mountain. Sudas heard it clearly. It was like the cracking of a great tree trunk in the instant before it fell.

You will be tempted to stop and stare up at the miracle that Indra wreaks. But if you do, it will cost you and your loved ones your lives. Ride, Sudas, ride! Do not be caught when Indra's vents his fury on the Ten Kings.

'Ride,' Sudas said aloud, his voice cracked and hoarse. 'Ride!' he said, more clearly, turning Saryu in a full circle, waving to Sudevi and his children and the others to make sure they all saw and heard him.

'RIDE!' he shouted, his voice drowned by a new burst of thunder, this one so deafening he felt as if the world itself would split open and swallow him whole.

19

Sudas and his small band were unobstructed as they rode across the timber bridge over the dammed Parusni River.

Every pair of enemy eyes were fixed either on the peak of Uttunga or closed in silent prayer. The events unfolding on the mountain peak had shocked every heart, and every mind was filled with a supernatural dread so great, none could function or move normally, not even to save their own skin.

He reached the far side and turned to make sure every last one of his people had crossed over successfully. As he did so, he noticed that the rampaging elephants had reached the outskirts of the cavalry and were now rioting through them. Armoured men and horses were being stamped down, gored with tusks or swatted aside as a hundred heads of grey madness swept through their lines. Hundreds of cavalrymen were killed for no reason but that they stood in the way of the rampaging elephants.

The beasts fought their way to the riverbank, not realising that there was only one bridge to cross. Reaching the edge of the Trtsu side, the frontrunners literally fell into the empty channel of the Parusni, tumbling into the empty riverbed. The elephants behind them followed, and the bodies piled up sickeningly fast. Some were able to get back to their feet and tried to scramble across to the far side, where they struggled to climb up the slippery silt of the bank.

But this was nothing compared to what was happening on Uttunga.

Sudas looked up at the mountain with a cold terror in his heart. Never in his wildest dreams had he imagined such a sight. It was a vision out of the most horrifying nightmare.

The mountain was being split open by lightning.

Bolt after bolt flashed down, until lightning was flowing in a seemingly endless stream of crackling white energy, a single near-continuous outpouring from the belly of the cloudbank.

Sudas shielded his eyes and glimpsed at the peak.

He could no longer see Guru Vashishta's silhouette and had no notion of what might have happened to the guru. Surely no one at such proximity to the barrage of Indra's vajras could have survived? He saw the yagna fire blazing in the Cradle of Agni. As he had suspected, it was fuelled by a great pile of wood. That was perfectly rational – Ambarish and the others had carried the wood up at the guru's request.

But there was something else on the peak that had not been there before, not even that morning.

It was a kind of pole or rod of some sort.

He could not make out exactly what it was, for the lightning was blinding now.

But whatever it was, it had attracted this onslaught of lightning since the fiery bolts were all directed towards it.

From its position and its proximity to the yagna fire, he knew it must be at the centre of the Cradle of Agni.

Something made him recall Guru Vashishta standing with his hands upraised, the staff in his right hand.

The staff in his right hand.

That in turn reminded him of how Guru

Vishwamitra had stood on the mountain top just this morning, with the staff in his right hand. The staff he had struck down upon the floor of the Cradle, shattering it and making a small peg-hole.

The hole that Guru Vashishta was trying so desperately to widen. He had even borrowed my dagger to do so.

Sudas knew instinctively that the rod or pole that was attracting the lightning was fixed into that hole.

And that the rod was joined to other similar rods that went below, far, far below the peak itself, into the very heart of the mountain. He did not know how he knew this, but he did. Something the guru had said, or referred to, made him glimpse this intuitively. It was not something he could explain in words, or even think out coherently, but he knew with a clear certainty that Guru Vashishta had imbedded those rods into the peak in order to attract the lightning somehow.

To call down Indra to our aid.

And now, Indra had responded to his devotee's plea. The lightning continued to flow down for a moment longer. Sudas lowered his gaze and saw the other Trtsus come riding across the river bridge with frantic haste.

He recognised Ucchasrava and waved to him. Ucchas rode up to him. Sudas noted that his lieutenant kept his eyes averted from Mount Uttunga and the phenomenon unfolding there. He realised that the man was witless with terror.

'Are you the last?' Sudas shouted, struggling to be heard over the incessant thunder which was now rolling in waves like a great waterfall battering a granite shelf. He had to repeat the words thrice before Ucchas understood.

The man shivered and nodded. 'I think...' was all Sudas heard before the thunder gnashed again.

Sudas pointed south. 'Ride! As fast as you can!'

He slapped the rump of Ucchasrava's horse, startling the poor animal, already terrified by the thunder and lightning.

Then he turned the head of Saryu as well. 'Ride!' he cried out, pointing to make sure everyone understood him.

They rode with him.

Behind himself, Sudas heard a new sound. A terrible epic gnashing and grinding. Again, it reminded him of the waterfall crashing onto granite. He heard screams and cries of outrage from across the bank and knew that the enemy was finally panicking. The first shock and paralysis were beginning to wear off and a realisation that something disastrous was about to happen was sinking in.

He saw Bolan just ahead, nursing an arrow in his shoulder and glancing back. The man's face was strained, either with the shock of the wound or what he was seeing, or both. 'The mountain!' he cried between bursts of thunder. 'It broke open like an egg!'

Sudas knew better than to look back. If he did that, Saryu would slow down, and he could not afford that.

'Ride!' he yelled, slapping Bolan's horse as he went past the man.

Behind him, he heard a great grinding sound even louder than the thunder, if such a thing were indeed possible.

The thunder had ceased entirely now. As had the lightning; Sudas did not need to look back to know this, he could tell by the absence of the flashes that had lit up the whole world a short while back.

The air was now pregnant with a stunning silence.

Sudas's ears rang as though the resonant thunder were swooping in to fill up the silence.

The world fell still and silent. Even the cries of

the elephants and horses, the screams of men and the barking of his dogs ceased.

Everyone and everything held its breath for one short moment.

And then all hell broke loose.

Sudas heard a sound like a dam bursting. He had heard one burst before, as a youth, and could never forget the sound.

This was just like that, but a thousand-fold.

This time, he could not resist and looked back.

Mount Uttunga had been split wide open by the lightning.

And a great body of water was gushing forth from within its depths. It gushed forth with the unmistakable force of a river in spate. Sudas could see white glacial water gleaming in the purple darkness, as it roared down the skirts of the mountain and washed into the plain.

The waves he saw, even at a distance, were so high, that even the tallest sala trees in the thicket, a good ten yards tall, were uprooted and washed away like mere twigs in a stream.

The water roared across the plain, washing trees, men, horses, elephants and chariots, filling the world with its relentless force, bearing all away in a swift terrible sweep.

After Indra broke the mountain, Varuna vents his rage!

Sudas saw the foaming seething waters reach the riverbank, and wash across. The timber bridge splintered as though made of sticks, and the riverbed filled with the gushing cascade.

And still the waters kept coming.

'RIDE!' Sudas yelled, racing Saryu past the others, knowing that her leadership would inspire the other horses to go faster. 'RIDE!' He glimpsed Sarama and the other dogs sprinting as well, putting on a final desperate burst of speed. The animals did not need to look back to know that death was pursuing them more relentlessly than any chariot, elephant or horse.

Sudas heard the water close in behind him, chasing them, roaring still with an unquenched fury. There was a moment when he thought they would be washed away as well. Then he heard the sound of stone beneath Saryu's hooves and felt the ground slope sharply upwards. He coaxed one final surge of effort from his mare, and moments later, rode up onto the top of the flatland that was often used by travellers to cross the great plain.

Do not stop until you have crossed the rocky road!

Sudas turned and looked down, pulling up some of the stragglers by hand and encouraging others.

He saw the water following, saw it approach within yards of where he stood, then saw it subside suddenly, without warning or cause, and fall back, bubbling and frothing.

By the grace of Indra, Varuna and Mitra, you and all your kind will be safe.

20

Using a thick cloth, Sudas slid the newly made brick out of the kiln. He could feel its searing heat even through the cloth. He tapped it against a granite stone and liked the solidity of the sound it made.

'This is a good brick,' he said to Indrani and Indraut.

They both clamoured to hold it.

He shook his head. 'Wait till it cools a little.'

He turned and showed it to the others. 'Our first brick!' he called out.

Everyone cheered loudly.

Ucchasrava grinned and came up to the kiln. 'May I take out the next one, Rajan?'

At once, the others began clamouring too. Salva, Assyr, Drahkyu, Parni and Kuruk wanted to hold the bricks. Sudas smiled wistfully as he showed them how to slide the hot freshly made bricks out of their slots, using a cloth to avoid burning their fingers. He missed seeing the faces of his other selectmen. The rest had all perished in the Battle of Ten Kings. Along with seventy score of the warriors.

He knew he should be grateful. It was a miracle that not one Trtsu had been killed by the cascading waters out of Uttunga. Even Guru Vashishta had survived. Apparently the guru had climbed down the mountainside while the lightning struck, and had known well enough to stay on the north face. Somehow he had clung on to a boulder even as the mountain split apart and unleashed its lethal load of water.

It was the guru who had explained the 'miracle' to Sudas privately afterwards. A tributary of the confluence of the three closest rivers had always run to ground within the mountain. There was a spring a mile farther south where the tributary sprang free again, but it was merely a brook, a bare trickle.

By damming the Parusni upstream, the Ten Kings had forced the river to divert towards the mountain. Somehow Guru Vashishta had known this, just as he had known the previous paths of the many rivers and tributaries that flowed through the land. He had known that after the torrential rains of the earlier days, the water diverted into the underground spring in Uttunga would be too much to be released through the tiny spring. It would bank, and continue to bank, until a great store of water collected within the mountain's belly.

All he had to do was release the water at the right time, to wash away the enemy forces.

And the way to do that had been shown to him by none other than Guru Vishwamitra himself.

That morning before the Battle of Dasarajna, when Guru Vishwamitra had struck his staff into the Cradle of Agni, he had inadvertently shown Guru Vashishta the precise point at which to imbed the rods.

Guru Vashishta had been collecting rods of iron over the past year with a mind to understanding the secrets of iron and how to work it. He had had their weapons made from the same store of iron by the same forgemaster – whose identity even Sudas did not know yet. That day, when Ambarish and the three hundred Trtsus had worked for Guru Vashishta, they had been ferrying rods of iron up Uttunga.

The guru had been making them push the rods through the hole in the Cradle – which was successively widened over the course of the day – until there was enough iron piercing the top of the mountain to make a solid pillar.

Lightning was attracted to iron. And to the highest point.

With his knowledge of the almanac, the guru was able to predict the weather to a precise point. He had known that around this time of the year, towards the end of the monsoon season, great thunderstorms raged and lightning flickered for hours in the night sky.

He had deduced, from his elaborate mental calculations, part of the great store of Vedic knowledge, that such a lightning storm would occur at precisely sundown on that day.

The fire was simple enough – man-made like any other yagna.

The invocation of Indra, Varuna and Mitra was a natural one too; afterall, they are the patron deities of the Trtsus.

The subsequent cracking of the mountain by the combined force of the lightning as well as the pressure of the water within was in a sense a feat of the devas – with just a little help from mere mortals.

Later, when Sudas had deemed it safe, he had returned to view the results.

Over sixty thousand enemy soldiers perished in the cascade. Not counting horses and elephants.

The army of the Ten Kings was wiped out completely.

The kings themselves were killed as well, for even though they were camped on the far bank, the water reached out and took them down. Anu and the remainder of his yoddha troops were gone. In fact, the Anus were almost entirely wiped out from the face of the earth, for every Anu had been present on the battlefield in a bid to regain their honour and pride after the first two defeats of the day.

Had there been any remaining resistance, it was quelled by the very fact that Sudas and the Trtsus had been able to summon Indra, Varuna and Mitra to their side.

The foreigners, those few that survived, had fled back to their homelands to report the extraordinary tale of the Battle of Ten Kings.

The Bharata tribes were united by the sheer force of the day's events.

Sudas had been unanimously acknowledged as samrat of the united Bharata tribes.

And today, he was about to lay the first brick of the first dwelling of the new Trtsu city.

He held up the brick again to show to the crowd that had gathered. All those who had left with the Anu earlier had returned, shamefaced and in tears. Sudas had forgiven them, for they had not gone to fight against him or the Trtsu but to be with their relatives in other tribes. He granted every last one of them immunity and unconditional acceptance.

Now he faced a gathering of over one score thousand. Twenty thousand Bharatas of every tribe, varna, creed and dialect. All assembled together, all proud first citizens of the new city and nation he was about to found.

He laid down the brick in the allotted spot, then raised his hands again to show they were empty, and that the task had been done.

A great roar of cheers greeted him.

Sudevi came up to him and embraced him warmly; Indrani and Indraut were close behind and hugged him from both sides. Sarama barked and jumped around them in a display of happiness.

'How does it feel to be emperor?' Sudevi asked him.

Sudas chuckled. 'It feels like I'm still adjusting to the

idea of being rajan! I have no idea what being a samrat really signifies. Do I grow five more pairs of hands? Or two more heads? I feel just the same. Still Sudas.'

'That is why you are a great king.'

'And you a great queen,' he said.

'I would like to be an emperor someday, Pitr,' Indraut said solemnly.

'Well, if you wish it, you must will it. Then you must work for it,' Sudas said. 'Perhaps you should start by being a good prince, then work your way upwards. If you are a successful king, you may someday become a great emperor too. How does that sound?'

'It sounds good, Pitr,' Indraut said, raising his chin in pride.

His sister rolled her eyes.

Both children ran after Sarama who was barking at something down the way.

Guru Vashishta approached. 'Samrat Sudas,' he said, emphasising the new title with evident relish. 'What do you wish to name your new city?'

Sudas had many names in mind. 'Is there an auspicious letter I should use to start the name?'

'The syllable Hu or Ha is auspicious,' Guru Vashishta suggested.

Sudas nodded slowly. 'I have a name that begins with that syllable.'

'What is it?' asked the guru.

'Harappa,' Sudas said.

The guru nodded approvingly. 'Harappa it is, then.'

Acknowledgements

Thanks are due to Vikas Rakheja and Manoj Kulkarni of Manjul Publishing House and Amaryllis Books for publishing this book, the first of my Itihasa Series. This one had an easier journey than my Ramayana Series and other mythological retellings. It only took me six years to find a publisher and another few years to see it published. That's quick compared to some of my other books! A special thanks to Rashmi Menon for editing the book and making the process so effortless.

And as always, thanks to you, the reader who feels as if my books are written especially for you, and as if I'm speaking directly into your heart and soul with certain lines, perhaps with all of them. You're right. I *am* writing for you. This book is for you as well. Because as the dedication to this book says, the song belongs to those who listen. Without you there to hear it, would there even be a song?